"Come in, Miss Summers, I've been waiting for you."

Dazed, Delia walked into an elegant, sun-filled office. Her worst nightmare had come true. Here was Craig Locksley. And now she knew that this meeting had always been inevitable. She'd been a fool to think she could escape him.

"Good morning, Mr. Locksley. I'm here from Orchid Cosmetics and—and—" Her confident manner faded. "I don't understand any of this. How can you possibly be here?"

"My partners have brilliant ideas, but not a lot of business sense. I provide that."

"I...get the picture," she said slowly.

"No, you don't. Your ideas of blindness come out of the nineteenth century. I have a computer that talks to me, a first-rate secretary and a mind that remembers everything."

"Everything?"

"Everything...."

From boardroom...to bride and groom!

Dear Reader,

Welcome to the latest book in our MARRYING THE BOSS miniseries, which features some of your favorite Harlequin Romance® authors bringing you a variety of tantalizing stories about love in the workplace!

Falling for the boss can mean trouble, so our gorgeous heroes and lively heroines all struggle to resist their feelings of attraction for each other. But somehow love always ends up top of the agenda. And it isn't just a nine-to-five affair.... Mixing business with pleasure carries on after hours—and ends in marriage!

Happy reading!

The Editors

Look out next month for a further novel in our
MARRYING THE BOSS series:
The Boss and the Baby by Leigh Michaels
Harlequin Romance #3552

Beauty and the Boss
Lucy Gordon

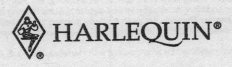

HARLEQUIN®

TORONTO • NEW YORK • LONDON
AMSTERDAM • PARIS • SYDNEY • HAMBURG
STOCKHOLM • ATHENS • TOKYO • MILAN • MADRID
PRAGUE • WARSAW • BUDAPEST • AUCKLAND

To The Guide Dogs for the Blind Association
with thanks for their help.

ISBN 0-373-03548-9

BEAUTY AND THE BOSS

First North American Publication 1999.

Printed in U.S.A.

CHAPTER ONE

'DELIA, DARLING!' The photographer advanced with his arms outstretched. 'Every time I see you, you're more beautiful. If only I could get some pictures of *you*, instead of those so-called models.'

Laughing, Delia tossed her mane of glorious black hair over her shoulder. 'Dear Max, you say that every time we meet.'

'I bet I'm not the only one who says it, either.'

It was true that Delia constantly received compliments about her looks. As assistant publicity director of Orchid Cosmetics she had the whole range of the firm's products at her disposal, but that was only part of the story.

Nature had made Delia gorgeous. She had large, dark eyes set in delicate, regular features, perfect skin and wavy black hair. Her body was tall and slender, with long, silky legs that short skirts showed off to perfection. She wasn't in the least vain about her beauty, but she knew that other people responded to it in a way that made them easy to deal with, and she'd unconsciously come to take this for granted.

Max snapped away busily at the models that had been hired to show off Orchid's new range. 'It's going to come out looking great,' he told her. 'The camera loves every lipstick and blusher, every grain of powder.'

'I hope you're right. Everyone's holding their breath about the new lines.'

Max dropped his voice. 'I hear that the publicity campaign has hit a few rough patches. Apparently the advertising agency you're using isn't up to scratch.'

'Hush!' she murmured, looking around. 'You know I can't tell tales out of school, Max.'

'Sweetie, the tales are telling themselves all over London. Lombard's is a rotten agency, and Brian won't admit it because he chose them. Not that he's exactly boasting about that. Has he managed to off-load the blame onto you yet?'

Delia laid a finger over her lips, but what Max said was true. Brian Gorham, chief publicity director of Orchid, had insisted on Lombard's and was distancing himself from the choice now. It was taking all Delia's skill to sidestep his attempts to put her in the firing line, but she was determined not to let him succeed. Brian would be retiring soon, and her heart was set on his job. She knew she was young for such a pro-motion, but her adventurous spirit had risen to the challenge. Her motto was Nothing ventured, nothing gained.

At last they were finished. The models, make-up experts and hairdressers began scurrying around in haste to leave the studio. Max sealed his films. 'Can I drive you home?' he asked Delia.

'No, thanks. I've just bought a new car and it's the love of my life.'

'That has a melancholy sound. Don't you ever long to love something warmer than a car?'

'You mean a man?' Delia asked with a chuckle.

'Whatever for? Cars are better. They don't argue and I get my own way all the time. Bye.'

The session had run late and it was dark as she made her way to the car park. Even in the dim light her new vehicle was perfect. Delia gazed adoringly at its sleek lines before sliding into the driver's seat. It had cost her more than she could afford, but it was worth it for the sense of achievement it gave her.

Despite what she'd said to Max it was only partly true that she prized her car above her boyfriend. For the past three months she'd been dating Laurence Davison, a handsome, youngish merchant banker. She was fond of him, but she hadn't fallen in love. Perhaps it was because he admired her looks too obviously, while seeming oblivious to the rest of her. It made her wonder if he saw her only as a status symbol.

She thought of Maggie, currently visiting her, with a heart of gold and a plain face, who'd said with the frankness of long friendship, 'Delia, if there's one thing about you that gets up my nose it's your ingratitude.'

'Ingratitude?' Delia had echoed, startled. 'Whatever do you mean by that?'

'I mean that if I looked like you I'd count my blessings, not witter on about wanting to be loved for myself.'

A few minutes into her journey Laurence called her on her mobile phone. Delia answered and pulled in to the side. She always felt safer that way.

'Just finished,' she said. 'On my way home now.'

'Meet me for supper?'

'Not tonight,' she said regretfully. 'I've got a report to write when I get home.'

'Did you really have to attend this photography session?' he asked. 'Couldn't you have stayed in the office and worked on your report?'

'Maybe,' she conceded reluctantly. 'But I really needed to be sure those pictures were just right. I've got to prove I'm good enough for that job.'

'Which means I'm not going to see you tonight,' he said peevishly.

'I'll make it up to you. Tomorrow?'

'I'll give you a call,' he said, and hung up abruptly.

There were a few more calls she needed to make. Leaving the car, she took the mobile to a small greasy spoon around the corner, ordered tea, and dialled the first number. By the time she'd finished she'd been there for half an hour. As she turned the corner outside she saw signs of a small commotion. A police car was a few feet from her own vehicle, and a large policeman was trying to placate the driver of a juggernaut. Both turned as Delia approached.

'Are you the owner of this car?' the policeman demanded.

'I am.'

'I've had a complaint.'

'About *me*?' Delia's voice was a masterpiece of innocent bewilderment.

'Yes, about you, from inside the factory whose gate your car is blocking. They work through the night, and their trucks need to get in and out.'

'I've got a home to go to,' the juggernaut driver said bitterly. 'And I'd like to dump this stuff and go to it, *if* no one minds.'

'Oh, goodness, I'm terribly sorry. How could I have been so thoughtless?' She smiled at the driver. 'I'll move at once.'

He gulped, taking in her breathtaking smile and large, glowing eyes. 'If you wouldn't mind, miss,' he said unsteadily.

'Don't go far,' the policeman said. 'I want a word.'

When she'd got out of the juggernaut's way she returned and gazed up to where the driver was now sitting in the cab. 'I do hope you forgive me.'

'Yeah—well, I may have been a bit hasty. No hard feelings, then, miss?'

'None at all.' She turned her head on one side in an angle she knew flattered her. He gulped again and turned his vehicle into the gate, narrowly missing the side.

The policeman snorted. 'That's all very well, Miss Summers—'

'How do you know my—? Oh, hello, Sergeant Jones. I remember now, we've met before.'

'Several times,' he agreed.

'Be fair,' she pleaded. 'I've never hurt anyone, and I'm completely sober. Why don't you get the Breathalyser out, and I'll prove it?'

'Just a minute. Your licence, please.'

Delia produced it at once.

'How about that Breathalyser?' she said as he studied it.

'All in good time.'

'But when I think of the burglars you could be apprehending, and all I want to do is blow into your little machine, and you won't let me—'

'Miss Summers,' he said patiently, 'you've got the

wrong script. *I'm* supposed to say, ''Will you blow into this, please?'' And *you're* supposed to say, ''Yes, Sergeant!'' You *don't* direct me here and there like a shepherd with an awkward sheepdog.'

She looked at him with wide, hurt eyes. 'Is that what I was doing? I'm really sorry.'

'Just blow into the machine,' he said patiently.

She did so and he studied the crystals intently, although both of them knew that the result would be negative.

'I never drink when I drive,' she declared truthfully. 'I don't know why you waste your time with me.'

He regarded her wryly. Detecting the hint of a twinkle far back in his eyes, Delia gave him the full benefit of her glorious smile. The sergeant breathed hard.

'I ought to charge you with causing an obstruction—'

'But you're not going to, are you? Not really.'

'Get out of here,' he said. 'And don't let me have to talk to you again.'

'Bless you!' She blew him a kiss.

'And that's enough of that,' he told her. 'Or I'll book you for trying to corrupt a police officer.'

He turned away, followed by her delightful chuckle, but before he reached the police car something made him stop and look back. 'Miss Summers!'

'Yes, Sergeant?'

'A word of advice. Be careful who you try it on. One day you'll meet a guy who's proof against it.'

'They don't live that long,' she told him cheerfully.

'You'll meet him. I just wish I could be there to

see it.' He gave her a friendly gesture of salute and got back into his car.

His words reminded Delia of her mother, who'd often said the same thing as she watched her daughter growing up enchanting men left, right and centre—starting with her father. It was a family legend how John Summers hadn't really wanted children, but had fallen under his baby daughter's spell on the first day.

Delia could remember being held up so that she could look directly into John's eyes, shining with adoration. 'Just wait till you're grown up!' he'd said. 'You're going to be a real heart-breaker. The boys'll be standing in line.'

It had happened just as he'd predicted. From wrapping John around her little finger it had been a short step to doing the same with every other man she met. Why not? It was so easy.

Delia might have become a spoilt brat. She was saved from that fate by a kind heart and a sense of the ridiculous. But she'd lived for twenty-four years in a world that was enchanted by her looks, and she knew nothing else.

After school she'd taken beauty courses and business courses, and had finally gone to work in the publicity department of a small cosmetics company. She'd learned her trade very thoroughly, and after two years she'd moved on to Orchid, a firm that had once dominated the cosmetics market, but then slumped when its image didn't keep up with the times.

It was thrilling. The whole firm was being reorganised. New products had been invented, and everything repackaged to look bright and modern. As assistant publicity director Delia was in the thick of the struggle to market Spring Dew for the teen market, Summer Bloom for the young-to-middle-aged customer, and Autumn Glow for the older woman. After three years things were going well, she reflected, but there was still much to do. She was so preoccupied with her thoughts that she failed to notice that her speed was creeping up and up.

Suddenly she realised what was happening. She stared in horror at the speedometer, only for a moment, but that moment was enough to cause disaster. In taking her eyes from the road she'd missed an approaching bend. She slammed on the brakes, wrenching frantically at the wheel. The car turned too sharply, and skidded around the bend with a shriek of tyres. Delia fought for control but she couldn't straighten the vehicle up again. Before she knew what was happening she'd mounted the pavement, and there was a sickening thump as she hit something.

At last she managed to stop, and was instantly out of the car and running back, praying desperately.

A man was on his knees, reaching out to a shape that lay slumped in front of him. Delia's heart lurched at the stillness of that shape. The man was calling a name in a desperate voice.

'Are you hurt?' she asked breathlessly, flinging herself down beside him.

'No, I'm fine,' he said quickly. 'But *she's* hurt— Jenny!—*Jenny!*'

Then Delia saw the dog lying there. She was a golden Labrador, a lovely animal with a large head and pale, silky fur. But she was frighteningly still.

'Oh, heavens!' Delia whispered. 'What have I done?'

'Is she dead?' the man asked raggedly. *'Is she dead?'*

Delia put her hand over Jenny's heart, and for the first time noticed that she was wearing the harness of a guide dog. Startled, she looked at the man and realised that his eyes were blank as he reached desperately for the animal.

To her great relief Delia could feel a heartbeat. 'She's alive,' she said, pulling herself together. 'If we get her to a vet quickly she'll be all right.' She was trying to reassure herself. Jenny's immobility scared her.

'Stay here,' she said. 'I'm going to fetch my car.'

She eased the car near to him and opened the rear door. He rose, gathering the dog carefully in his arms. Jenny whimpered.

'Here,' Delia said, guiding him to the door. 'A little more to the right—let me hold her while you get in.'

'No,' he said with soft vehemence. He added raggedly, 'She's uneasy with strangers.'

But Delia understood his real meaning. After what she'd done he didn't want her touching Jenny. She closed the door after them and quickly got into the driving seat.

'Tell me where to go,' she said.

He gave her the name of his vet, and the night telephone number, which she called. 'We'll be there in ten minutes,' she informed the vet.

'Who am I to expect?' he asked.

'What's your name?' she asked her passenger.

'Craig Locksley,' he said in a hoarse voice. 'Tell them it's Jenny.'

'Mr Locksley is bringing Jenny.'

She was practically functioning on automatic as she drove. If she'd allowed herself to think she would have been consumed by guilt. She'd been speeding, however unintentionally, and through her own carelessness she'd knocked down a guide dog. The sight of Jenny drooping in her master's arms had almost overcome her. She'd pulled herself together so that she could be of some use, and now she was fighting to keep calm.

Don't let her die, she prayed silently.

To her relief they arrived to find a door already open and the vet standing waiting for them. He and a nurse brought a trolley out to the car, lifted Jenny onto it and hurried in. Craig Locksley stood by the car, looking desperate.

'Can I help you get inside?' Delia asked.

'No, thank you!'

'But—'

'I know the layout of this place,' he said coldly. 'All you can do for me is get out of the way. In fact, leave altogether. There's nothing further for you to do.'

She stood aside and he made his way carefully to the door. Apparently he really did know the layout, because he turned in the right direction. Delia followed him inside to the brightly lit room where Jenny lay on the table. The vet was removing the harness and talking to Craig Locksley.

'A car, you say? Any idea how fast it was travelling?'

'Yes,' Delia said, and told him what had happened.

The vet pursed his lips. 'Bad,' he said. 'All right, it's best if you two wait outside. I'll do what I can.'

The man reached out to touch Jenny. At that moment she came round and raised her head to lick him. The love and trust between them was almost tangible.

'It's all right, old girl,' he whispered against her golden fur. 'I'm here.'

Jenny caressed his face with her tongue, and thumped her tail feebly. Delia looked away to hide the fact that her eyes had suddenly blurred.

'Is there somewhere I can clean up?' she asked, and the nurse guided her to the little washroom.

She was grimy from having knelt in the road. As she washed she found she was shaking. What she'd done was bad enough, but to it was added the contempt in the man's voice when he'd rejected her services. She couldn't blame him, but it was vital to speak to him again, and make him understand that she wasn't as bad as he thought.

She found him sitting in the waiting room, his head leaning back against the wall, his eyes closed. He was younger than she'd first supposed, probably in his early thirties, with a lean face that was set in a harsh look of grief and despair. She had no chance to study him further because when he heard her he sat up, immediately alert.

'I told you to go,' he said sharply. 'Nobody needs you here.'

'But—I have responsibilities, Mr Locksley. I've caused you injury—at least you must let me tell you my name, and give you my insurance details.'

He turned his head, and although she knew he couldn't see her the look of scorn he flung in her direction made her flinch.

'And what is your insurance company going to do

if my friend dies?' he demanded harshly. 'Bring her back to life?'

'Your—friend?'

'You'd probably call her just a dog. What would you know about it? For seven years Jenny has given me her love and her unquestioning loyalty. She spends her life controlling her natural instincts so that she can put me first. She keeps me safe. She's there in the night. She's honest and she's *warm.*' His voice was husky.

'I'm sorry,' she faltered.

'To hell with you!' he raged. 'You're sorry! You took that bend at an insane speed—yes, I knew you were speeding long before you arrived. I could hear it. Jenny heard it. She wouldn't step into the road, but then you mounted the pavement, so she didn't have a chance. She put herself between me and your car—' He stopped and shuddered. Delia watched him in horror. 'Now she's probably dying,' he resumed after a moment. 'And you're *sorry.*'

Delia was silent. There was nothing to say in the face of so much anguish.

'Well, go on,' he sneered. 'Aren't you going to recite the next bit?'

'What—?'

'Your smooth speech about how you'll cover all the vet's bills. After all, you're a very prosperous woman. Cars that hum as sweetly as yours cost a fortune. So you'll pay my bills and think that settles it.'

'No,' she said quickly. 'At least—of course I will, but I'm not so insensitive as to say it now. You said it, not me. Why can't you give me a chance?'

'How much chance did Jenny have?'

'She won't die—I'm sure she won't. I saw a mass of advanced equipment in the vet's surgery—and there's so much they can do these days—'

'You know nothing about it,' he said flatly. 'Words to make yourself feel better won't help Jenny.'

'No, they won't. I'm sorry, I was just—'

'I know what you were trying to do. Please go now.'

'No,' she said with sudden resolution. 'This concerns me too. I'm staying until I know how she is.'

'And if I say I don't want you to, that makes no difference, does it? You've decided, and that's it, because you're the kind of woman who always does what she wants.'

'You know nothing about the kind of woman I am.'

'I would have said I know quite a lot, and none of it does you credit,' he said with bitter irony. 'You have a very high opinion of yourself. You drive fast because you expect the world to get out of your way. And you have an impatient face.'

Hot anger sprang to her lips, but she forced it back. 'Mr Locksley, I don't want to be offensive, but you don't know what my face looks like,' she said.

'Your voice is impatient. If your face doesn't reflect it yet, it soon will.'

No one had spoken to Delia like that for as long as she could remember. Whatever her mistakes she'd always been able to win swift forgiveness. But not from this man. Her beauty, the magic talisman she'd always relied on, meant nothing to him.

'I know you're angry with me,' she tried again. 'But I did my best to put it right. I got Jenny here as fast as I could.'

'Yes, I appreciate that you're not a hit-and-run driver,' he responded in a tone of cool dismissal. 'There are plenty of people who'd simply have driven off. Just as there are plenty of people who wouldn't have hit her in the first place.'

It was hopeless. She couldn't win against his implacable judgement. Delia rose and walked out of the waiting room, unable to bear his rage and contempt. It was better to wait outside until she knew Jenny's fate.

There was a chill in the night air, but she was hardly aware of it. She felt as if she'd had a blow in the stomach. It was like becoming another person, one who could actually do something as terrible as this. She wanted to protest that this other self wasn't really her. But it was. She hated the sensation, and she wasn't sure she could cope with it.

The door opened behind her and he stood there.

'What are you doing out here?' he demanded.

'How did you—?'

'For pity's sake! It's not a conjuring trick! I didn't hear your car leave, but I could still hear your footsteps. When you stormed off I thought you'd gone for good.'

'I didn't storm off,' she protested. 'I left to relieve you of my hated presence.'

'Come inside and stop being melodramatic,' he snapped.

Having invited her in, he showed no further interest in her, but sat with his hands clasped between his knees, staring sightlessly into space. Delia found herself trying to study him without being too obvious about it, just as she would have done with a sighted person. He seemed intensely aware of everything about him, and she couldn't help feeling that if she looked at him he would know.

Craig Locksley was a handsome man: tall, with wide shoulders and an athletic build. He had dark, brilliant eyes that showed no sign of blindness. His face was lean, with vivid features and a wide, shapely mouth. There was sensitivity in that mouth, but also bitterness, she thought. She wondered how it looked when he laughed. Or did he never laugh? Had the bitterness so invaded his soul that there was no room for tenderness or joy?

She had some sort of answer a moment later, when there was the shrill of a mobile phone. He took a phone from his pocket. 'Yes?' he asked sternly.

The next moment his face had relaxed into a smile. 'Hello, darling,' he said warmly. 'Are you having a good time?'

Delia tried not to listen, but in the quiet waiting room it was impossible to avoid hearing. The man's face was transformed by love.

'I know I'm usually at home by now,' he said, 'but Jenny and I took our walk a little late tonight... Yes, she's fine...and I'm fine... No, of course I don't want you to hurry home...give my love to them both... Bye.'

As soon as he'd finished his face altered dramatically, revealing the strain of putting on a bright front when the truth was tearing him apart. Delia wondered who 'darling' was, and why he was so protective of her.

At that moment the door to the surgery opened, and

the vet appeared. Jenny's fate seemed to be written all over his weary face.

'That's that,' he said heavily.

CHAPTER TWO

THEY both froze in horror, while the dreadful finality of 'That's that' tolled like a death knell.

'One of the toughest jobs I've ever done,' the vet said. 'But it's finished now, and she's very strong, despite not being as young as she was.'

Delia stared, hardly daring to hope. 'You mean—?'

'She's not out of the woods yet, but she's got through the worst. Now it's just a question of waiting.'

Craig was very pale and seemed to be holding himself in check with great control. 'Thank you,' he said with an effort. 'Thank you.'

'Go home now,' the vet advised him.

'Yes,' he said unsteadily. 'I'd better go in case Alison calls the house phone and finds me out. I haven't told her—I let her think everything was fine. I don't know how I'll explain if—'

'It probably won't happen,' the vet said firmly.

'But you can't be sure, can you?' Delia asked.

'Not yet. She's got a good chance, but she has some nasty injuries. Shall I call you a cab?'

'There's no need,' Delia said. 'I'll drive Mr Locksley home.'

He left the surgery with her. Not until they were well out of the vet's hearing did he say curtly, 'I'll get myself home. Goodnight.'

21

'Won't you please let me drive you?' she begged.

'It's quite unnecessary, thank you. I'm very familiar with these roads.'

He strode off down the road, moving so easily that Delia thought he might really manage alone. But suddenly he stopped. She saw him turn and reach out, feeling the hedge on one side of him, and a lamppost on the other. It was obvious that he'd become disorientated.

Delia caught up in the car, and got out to confront him. 'Mr Locksley, I'm sorry for all I've done, but I am simply not going to abandon you to walk home alone. Please get into my car. You don't have to forgive me, or even talk to me. Just don't add more damage to what I've already caused.'

He steadied himself against the lamppost. His whole attitude spoke of tension and anguish. Delia ventured to touch him, but he stiffened at once and she snatched her hand back. She opened the rear door, letting it click as audibly as she could.

'The car's just in front of you,' she said. 'The door's open. All you have to do is get in.'

Now she could hear herself as he obviously heard her—an impatient woman who gave orders. No doubt his poor opinion of her was reinforced.

He stood motionless for so long that she thought he would refuse, but at last he reached out. When he was sure it was the rear door he'd found, he got in. Delia bitterly appreciated his manoeuvres to make sure he didn't have to sit next to her.

'Can I have your address, please?' she asked as she got into the driving seat. When he'd given it she added, 'Shall I call your home in case they're worried about you?'

'There's nobody there.'

'You live alone?'

'No, I don't live alone—if it's any concern of yours. I live with my daughter, but she's away visiting her grandparents, thank goodness.'

After a few minutes she turned into a tree-lined street. His home surprised her. She'd pictured a small, neat flat, adapted for a blind person, but he lived in a large Victorian house, set back from the road. It looked rambling and comfortable.

'Thank you,' he said, getting out. 'Goodnight.'

'Not yet,' she said firmly. 'I'm going to fix you a stiff drink.'

He took a long, exasperated breath. 'Is there any way of getting rid of you?'

'Yes,' she said with spirit. 'Let me come in and see that you're all right. Try to believe that I'm really sorry. Talk to me for a while. Then I'll leave quietly.'

'Very well! On those terms.'

He was a different man in his own domain. He climbed the four steps to the front door and put the key in the lock without hesitating. At his signal Delia passed in front of him into the house and turned just in time to see him stand aside for an unseen presence. He checked himself with a sharp breath, and Delia's hand flew to her mouth as she realised that he'd instinctively made room for Jenny. But Jenny wasn't there. She was lying sedated in a darkened room, fighting for her life. He remembered it too, and his face had a withered look.

'Come in,' he said curtly.

He flicked on the light switches and showed her into a large room that looked like a library. Books lined two of the walls. A third wall was covered in posters, and the fourth was taken up by a huge bay window. A desk in the corner held a computer that Delia could see was state-of-the-art. In the centre of the room was a leather sofa. There were a couple of leather armchairs and several very large cushions scattered about. The colour scheme was autumnal, a mixture of brown, orange, biscuit and tan that was both warm and restful.

He made his way to the drinks cabinet in the corner and poured himself a stiff brandy.

'None for you,' he declared. 'You've got to drive home. You'd better have a hot drink. You've had a shock. Tea or coffee?'

'Coffee, please. Can I help?'

'Thank you, but I know my way around my own kitchen.' He left the room.

After a moment she followed him. The kitchen was bright and modern, with every possible gadget. He moved as easily as a sighted man, putting his hand on precisely placed objects. Some of the containers made her smile. They were shaped like comic animals, and struck a strange note with this stern man.

'Most of this is my daughter's doing,' he said, hearing her approach. 'It was her idea to use the animal containers. I protested a bit, but I can always tell exactly what I've got hold of, from the feel. The bear is sugar, the squirrel is tea, and the penguin is coffee. Take this inside.'

He handed her the tray and signalled for her to move on. His manner was authoritative, even brusque, and Delia had the feeling this wasn't just because he could relax in his own home. Instinct told her that this was the real Craig Locksley. His earlier hesitation had simply been due to his disorientation. Nature had designed him to command.

'Put the tray on that low table,' he said, 'and sit in the armchair by the lamp.'

'What difference does it make where I sit?' she demanded, becoming a bit nettled.

'It's a question of acoustics,' he said, settling himself on the sofa. 'For some reason they're clearer in that precise spot.'

'You mean it's your equivalent of turning a lamp onto my face?' she said wryly.

He gave a sudden grin, and it transformed him. 'Exactly,' he said. 'You must allow me my occasional small advantages.'

A moment later he proved how sharp his hearing was. Delia's attention was taken by a photograph on the table. She turned it towards her, the frame making a faint scratching noise. At once he said, 'That's my daughter, Alison. She's ten.'

Delia was immediately drawn to the impish little girl who sat with her arm flung around a beaming Labrador.

'The dog with her—' she began.

'Yes, that's Jenny. Alison adores her. That's why I didn't tell her anything when she called me tonight.'

The accusation hung in the air between them. To fend it off, Delia said quickly, 'She's lovely.' This was stretching the facts rather. The child looked intelligent and full of personality, but her face wasn't conventionally pretty, although it had promise for later.

'Yes, she is lovely,' he answered. 'But how would you *know*?'

'Well—I can see—' she stammered.

'Yes, you can see, but how do you know? How do you think *I* know? I've been blind for years. I haven't seen her since she was small, but I know that she's beautiful. Her heart is kind and gentle. Her soul is loving. She has grace and compassion.'

'Things that you don't believe I know anything about?' Delia challenged.

He was silent.

'What about your wife?' Delia asked when she couldn't bear it any longer.

His mouth tightened. 'I'm divorced,' he said curtly.

'And now Alison looks after you?'

'*I* look after *her*,' Craig snapped. 'Just like any other father.'

'I'm sorry,' Delia said, mortified. 'Everything I say seems to be wrong.'

'Only because you're looking at life the wrong way,' he said.

'I obviously don't look at it in your way,' she said. 'How can I? You live in a different kind of world—'

'No,' he interrupted her. 'I live in the same world that you do. But it reaches me in different ways. Drink your coffee. I make very good coffee.'

The abrupt change of subject disconcerted her. While she sipped the excellent coffee he said, 'You'd better tell me about yourself. What's your name?'

Evidently he was a man who'd never heard the word 'please', she thought.

'My name is Delia Summers,' she began.

'You sound as if you're in your twenties,' he said, with a question in his tone.

'Yes, I am.'

'Does the car belong to you?'

'When I've finished paying the instalments, yes.'

'Then you're successful in your job. What is it?'

'I'm the assistant publicity director for Orchid Cosmetics.'

'And you want your boss's job.'

'Don't tell me you can hear that as well?' she said with an edge in her tone.

'Of course. Why not? Ambition is a quality that comes across very clearly. You're efficient, and you know where you're going.'

'Except when I drive,' Delia added with a sigh.

'I purposely didn't say that. Go on about yourself. What do you look like?'

'I'm tall, slim. I have very long legs, long black hair and dark blue eyes.'

He gave a faint grin. 'And you're used to men telling you that you're beautiful.'

'That was a guess,' she insisted.

'No, it wasn't. You listed your assets lovingly. You're proud of them. From your footsteps I'd say you have high heels to set off those legs that you couldn't resist telling me were *very* long. You're probably wearing a short skirt as well so that everyone can see and admire them.'

'I have to look my best in my job,' Delia said. 'Otherwise I wouldn't be much of an advertisement for Orchid Cosmetics.'

As she said this she instinctively put her head on

one side as she'd done with the truck driver. It emphasised her long neck, and made her hair swing free in glorious curves. It was most effective when combined with a half smile and a direct look through her heavy lashes. It was her automatic response when dealing with a man she wanted to win over, and it was basically as innocent as a puppy wagging its tail for approval. But when she found herself doing it now a wave of self-disgust went through her.

She glanced nervously at Craig Locksley, who seemed to know everything without being told. Would he detect her foolish attempt to charm him with her beauty, and despise her even more for it?

'Go on,' he said. 'Why have you stopped talking?'

'There's nothing more to say about me.'

'Strange. You might have told me if you're married, and whether you have children. But it never crossed your mind, did it?'

'Why don't *you* tell *me*?' she asked tensely. 'I'm sure something in my voice has already given you the answer.'

'You have no children. In fact you have no responsibilities to anyone but yourself.'

'Now there you're wrong. I have a lot of responsibility in my job—'

'Job,' he said impatiently. 'I'm talking about human responsibility—people. You've never borne a child or even cared for one. You've never loved another creature more than yourself.'

'Who would have thought my voice revealed so much?' Delia said after a little silence. If only she could get out of here, away from this man who disliked and disapproved of her. But to go now would feel like running away, and she was no quitter.

'Your choice of job reveals a great deal more,' he observed. 'But then, if you find the surface of life so agreeable, it's natural to choose to work with surfaces.'

'Well, surfaces matter,' she retorted. 'Not to you, perhaps, but to the rest of us. Of course women want to be pretty. Why blame them for it? Why not blame the men who put a premium on beauty?'

'Not all men,' he countered sharply.

'But how many are like you?'

'Not many are blind,' he agreed. 'But plenty of the sighted ones know that Shakespeare was right when he said, A fair face will wither...but a good heart is the sun and the moon. That's *Henry V* in case you want to look it up.'

'Thank you,' she said angrily. 'How kind of you to enlighten my ignorance. Now let me enlighten yours. These sensitive male creatures, looking into people's souls, are figments of your imagination. Most men look at a woman's face and figure.'

'I dare say you'd know about that,' he said affably. 'Beauty is quite a weapon, isn't it?'

'Yes,' she said defiantly.

'Tell me, have you ever had to face up to anything in your entire life? Or have those very long legs and black hair always taken care of things for you?'

'I've had enough of this,' she said angrily. 'The accident was my fault, but it doesn't entitle you to make glib judgements about me. You don't believe it, but I'm really sorry. I'd do anything to undo what I've done. Oh, I know what you're thinking—'

'Do you?'

'Yes—that it can't be undone, and I'm just trying to make myself feel better—'

'Am I as hard as that?' he murmured.

Delia hardly heard him. She'd held herself in check, but now the shock and strain were getting to her. She set her cup down sharply, jumped up and began to stride restlessly about the room.

'You don't have to tell me,' she told him. 'I know it's true. I hate myself, but what can I *do*? I'm not really the kind of person who does things like this— Oh, yes, it's easy to claim that afterwards, isn't it?'

'Is that another of the things I was going to say?' he asked wryly.

'Perhaps you're right. Perhaps I *am* this kind of person—stupid and selfish, and oblivious to everyone except myself. But I don't mean to be. I'd give anything to put the clock back to just before it happened—'

It was suddenly too much for her. She heard her voice wobble and tried to fight back the tears, but she couldn't blot out the sense of horror. She stood with her arms crossed over her breast, fighting for control.

He was on his feet, moving the two steps towards her, taking hold of her. She tried to push him away, furious with herself for yielding to weakness, but his hands were strong. He put one arm firmly around her shoulder.

'Come and sit down,' he said.

'No, just leave me—I'll be all right—'

'I said, sit down, and don't argue.' He pulled her down onto the sofa beside him. 'That's better,' he said firmly. 'Come on, there's no need for you to cry.'

'I'm not—crying,' she said in a gasping voice.

'You sound on the verge of hysterics.'

'I'm *not*,' she said fiercely. 'How dare you say that?'

Her mind kept playing and replaying the moment of the collision, the sight of Jenny lying on the ground, the way her body had drooped when he'd raised her. It came to an end, went back to the beginning and started again.

'No!' she said huskily. 'Not again. *Please*—I didn't mean to—'

She couldn't say any more. She was heaving with sobs that wouldn't be forced back. She tried to pull out of his arms but he drew her closer while the storm of anguish raged within her. His movements were neither rough nor gentle. They were simply matter-of-fact. But his chest was broad and firm, and a curious sense of comfort began to steal over her. He despised her, but the power of his arms seemed to promise that the world could be a safe place after all.

'What did you mean—not again?' he asked.

'I keep seeing what happened—I try not to—my mind keeps going over and over it. If you only knew—'

'But I do. My mind does exactly that, and I can't escape by looking at my surroundings. It won't last. You're in a state of shock, but it'll pass soon enough.'

'You think I'm pretty shallow, don't you?'

'Let's say I don't think you're used to having to deal with unpleasantness. Now you've got to, and it's far more of a shock to you than anything you've done.'

'That isn't true,' she protested hotly.

'Isn't it? Well, maybe I'm wrong about you.'

'But you don't think so?' she demanded, stung by his dismissive tone.

He shrugged. 'Does it really matter? We met by accident, and we'll forget each other in an hour. Why should either of us care about the other's opinion?'

'No reason at all,' she said in a muffled voice.

'You're not still crying, are you? Now that's enough.' He spoke in a bracing voice, and produced a clean handkerchief, which he used to dry her cheeks. His brilliant eyes seemed to be focused directly on her. Despite their lack of expression it was almost impossible to believe that he couldn't see.

Delia felt confused. Men had studied her face before, with delight. But there was no admiration in this man's eyes. There was nothing at all. And yet...

She saw the moment when his attention was arrested. His movements slowed, and he seemed to forget what he'd started out to do. He dropped the handkerchief, and began to explore her features with his fingers. She held her breath as he softly touched her eyes, her nose, her mouth. He seemed to be lost in a dream. The strength and warmth of his hands affected her strangely. At last an almost imperceptible sigh broke from him. He lowered his hands.

'I apologise,' he said harshly. 'I had no right to do that without asking you first. Forgive me.'

'It's all right,' she said, trying to speak normally. 'I just hope you discovered what you wanted to know.'

'A good deal. You have splendid bone structure, and delicate, regular features. It's a good beginning.'

'A beginning?'

'It creates the superficial appearance of beauty, but it won't last long if you go on destroying it the way you're doing.'

This was such a let-down after what had just happened that Delia replied angrily, 'That's nonsense. I have the whole of Orchid Cosmetics to choose from, and I use everything necessary to take care of my looks.'

'Ah, yes,' he said ironically. 'Moisturisers, and softening creams, and skin food—things you put on at night and take off in the morning, and other things that you put on in the morning and take off at night. Do you really think I meant *that*?'

'Now look—'

'No, you look! Or, more importantly, feel. Put your finger tip between your eyebrows. Feel the little frown-line there. All the wrinkle removers in the world aren't going to erase that line as long as you're busy deepening it every day.

'You don't laugh enough, not really laugh. You smile politely, but you don't let yourself go with spontaneous laughter. That would make your face lighter, because it takes fewer muscles to laugh than to frown. Did you know that? Come down from your pedestal and join the rest of the world. Then perhaps the line will start to fade.'

'Well, you've got a nerve—'

'Why, because I dare to criticise you? Perhaps if you'd heard more of the harsh truth about yourself my friend might not be lying at death's door. You live in a world of surfaces, and mostly you arrange them to your own satisfaction.'

'I'm not listening to another word,' Delia said angrily. 'This is all speculation. You don't know half of the things about me that you pretend to know—'

'How can you tell what I know and don't know? Can you get behind my useless eyes and sense what's there? If you could, you might have a shock. I don't understand beauty as you mean it. What I understand best is the inner truth that lies hidden in everything.'

'Perhaps you don't judge people's inner truth as accurately as you think,' she said tensely. 'You're so sure you know *my* inner truth. Impatient and domineering. Isn't that how you see—imagine me?'

'You can say the word 'see',' he told her wryly. 'I won't fall apart.'

'But that's how you think of me, isn't it?' she insisted. 'Impatient and domineering?'

'Impatient and unhappy,' he said quietly.

'Nonsense! I'm not unhappy.'

'I think a lonely woman is always unhappy.'

'What about a lonely man?' she threw at him.

'I wouldn't know. I'm not lonely. I have my daughter to love. But who do you love?'

'I don't love anyone,' Delia said with a touch of defiance. 'But I have plenty who love me.'

'So why are you lonely?'

'I've told you, I'm *not*.'

'Then why do you sound haunted and desperate?'

'You imagined that, and I'm not continuing this conversation. You know nothing about me. *Nothing*.'

She pulled away from him and got hastily to her feet. As she moved away he reached out for her.

'Wait!' he cried.

'I'm leaving my card on the desk beside your computer. Please let me know how much I owe you for Jenny's care. Now it's time I was going.'

'Not yet.'

'It's very late and I have a lot to do when I get home,' Delia said brightly. She wanted to run far away from this place, from this man with his eyes that saw nothing and everything.

'You can't go like this,' he said, rising to his feet. *'Delia!'*

Only later would she realise that he'd used her first name for the only time that night. All she could think of at that moment was escaping him. She almost ran to the front door, and the next moment she was out in the street.

CHAPTER THREE

'AND I couldn't bear the thought that I'd done a thing like that.'

'It probably wasn't your fault at all,' Laurence said soothingly.

'Of course it was. I was speeding, and that poor dog—'

'I thought guide dogs were supposed to protect their owners,' Laurence said coolly and with the merest hint of boredom. 'It couldn't have been doing its job properly.'

'Jenny isn't an "it". She's a she. I mounted the pavement—'

'Waiter, another bottle of wine.'

'I'm sorry if I've been boring you,' Delia said stiffly.

'Let's just say that I'm more interested in telling you how beautiful you are tonight. Of course, that's always true—'

'But what do you mean when you say it, Laurence? That my features are regular and my nose straight? Is that all beauty is?'

'I beg your pardon?' he said blankly.

'Shouldn't it have something to do with what's inside?'

He kissed her hand. 'Who cares for what's inside? I'll settle for the exquisite exterior.'

Delia frowned. 'Perhaps that's what he meant,' she murmured.

'Who?'

'Never mind.' She checked herself hastily. 'It's just that I've been doing some thinking.'

'I know you have,' he said with a sigh. 'When you're not fretting about this fellow and his wretched dog you're going off at philosophical tangents about inner meaning. You never used to be like this.'

'I know. I feel as if I'm never going to be the same person again.'

They were sitting in a very expensive restaurant in the heart of London's Mayfair. Laurence liked to show Delia off in luxurious surroundings. Tonight she was wearing an olive-green silk dress that displayed her smooth, perfect shoulders, and about her neck was a ruby pendant. Heads had turned as they'd entered, and other men had regarded Laurence with envy. It was the kind of evening they'd often spent together in perfect harmony. But tonight something was wrong.

In fact, something had been wrong every night for the last month. As Delia had driven away from Craig's house she'd felt relieved to think that he was growing distant, fading into nothing. But when she'd reached home he'd seemed to be there, waiting for her. Her exquisite apartment, her carefully chosen possessions had all looked different, as though a man who couldn't see had changed the lighting.

Next day she'd called the vet, and discovered, to her heartfelt relief, that Jenny was still holding on. But her attempt to pay the bills had been turned down. The receptionist had explained that Craig Locksley had insisted on paying every penny himself. He'd even gone to the lengths of leaving firm instructions that the vet mustn't take any money from her.

And that was no more than I expected, Delia thought wryly.

Since then she'd called twice more, and gathered that Jenny was out of danger and recovering slowly. Now, she'd thought, she really would be able to put it behind her.

A crisis at work was demanding all her attention. Gerald Hedwin, the firm's managing director, had cancelled the contract with Lombard's, the disastrous agency, and quietly made it clear to Delia that he knew Brian was to blame.

But Brian had fought back at a big publicity meeting. He'd arrived with a smooth young man called Mark, whom he'd introduced as his nephew, 'seconded to the department'. It was the first Delia had heard of it. During the meeting Brian had lost no chance to push Mark forward, and it had been clear that he had him lined up as his successor.

Mark's appearance was smooth, like his ideas and his presentation. The managing director had seemed impressed. Only Delia had been troubled by a certain slick coldness about the young man.

'For a new advertising agency we could do a lot worse than look at Calloways,' Mark said. 'They're aggressive and go-getting, and some of their recent results have been very impressive. Norrington Groceries have recently doubled their turnover, and they ascribe it to the brilliant campaign Calloways mounted.'

He thrust a folder across the table at Mr Hedwin,

who studied it, giving small grunts of agreement. Delia saw Mark and Brian exchange gleeful looks. A glance at the folder showed her that the work was excellent, but she was dismayed at the way she'd been deliberately sidelined.

'Actually I'd have liked to bring them on board before,' Brian said, 'but they couldn't take us. They're very much in demand. But Mark has connections in the firm and he's been pulling strings for us.'

'Well done, Mark,' Mr Hedwin said, beaming.

Delia could see the job slipping away from her, unless she could come up with something good.

'Well, if that's everything—' Mr Hedwin began to say.

'Actually, there is one more thing,' Delia said quickly. 'I think I've found a new approach. I'd like to write some leaflets to be distributed with our goods—'

Brian laughed patronisingly. 'Tips on how to put on lipstick, the latest technique for blusher and foundation. Good solid stuff, of course, but hardly original.'

'I didn't mean just make-up techniques,' Delia said. 'I'm talking about *inner* beauty—the true beauty of the heart that creams and lotions can never replace.'

'Once women start thinking along those lines, who needs us?' Mark demanded.

'They do, if we tackle it properly,' Delia said at once. 'Look, we all know that a good complexion starts with a good diet. If a woman is eating the wrong things creams won't give her a perfect skin. Beauty comes from within physically, but also spiritually.'

'But who's interested?' Mark objected. 'Women

make up to attract men, because they realise that men care most about their looks.'

'Actually,' Delia retorted, 'there are plenty of men who know that Shakespeare was right when he said, "A fair face will wither...but a good heart is the sun and the moon."' She saw that Mark was looking taken aback, and added casually, 'That's *Henry V* in case you want to look it up.'

'Shakespeare, eh?' Mr Hedwin mused. 'I like it. It's classy. Go on.'

'No lotion will keep wrinkles at bay in someone who's constantly frowning,' Delia said, warming to her theme. 'Did you know that it takes more muscles to frown than to smile? We've already put out advisory leaflets on health and diet. I'd like to write some about improving your appearance with a beautiful nature.'

'Fine,' Mr Hedwin said, 'but how are you going to translate this into extra sales?'

Delia gave him her best confident smile. 'By the way I write them.'

'Then let me see something soon.'

'I worked really hard on those leaflets,' Delia told Laurence now, as they sat over their coffee and liqueurs. 'And they came out well.'

'So what's wrong?' Laurence asked, for something in her tone proclaimed her dissatisfaction.

'It's him,' she said restlessly. 'Craig Locksley. The whole thing came from him, and I didn't even see it until it was too late.'

'You discussed the leaflets with him?'

'No, I mean all that stuff about inner beauty was

his. I thought I'd been so original, and I was just parroting him.'

She didn't add that the real shock had been the discovery that she hadn't dismissed him from her mind at all. He'd been there, silently haunting her, all the time.

'Well, that's how to succeed in this world,' Laurence said comfortably. 'Take something from everyone you meet. I shouldn't have to tell *you* that.'

'Meaning that I'm a taker?' Delia asked, shocked. 'Just a taker, not a giver?'

'Hey, steady on. I only meant that you've always had that beautiful head screwed on right.'

Delia smiled mechanically. Somehow she couldn't enjoy compliments any more, and this particular compliment made her uneasy. Soon afterwards she announced that she had a headache and asked Laurence to take her home.

When her door was safely locked behind her she stripped and showered, trying to disperse something that seemed to cling to her from the restaurant. It was an atmosphere of heat and over-indulgence, of senses gorged on food, wine and the promise of heedless pleasure. It was familiar, and it had never troubled her before. But tonight she needed to wash it away.

She thought about her recent success. She'd written the leaflets in a blaze of inspiration. The words had poured out:

You've made a good start by choosing Orchid's Skin Lotion, but watch yourself in the mirror as you rub it in. Are you frowning over the troubles of the day? Forget them. Bickering with your husband

will only increase the lines you're trying to banish.
Forgive him if he didn't put the rubbish out.
Concentrate on the kind things he's done for you.
You'll be happier, and you'll be helping Orchid to
help you.

There were six leaflets, each one written like that,
with a subtle twist that made inner beauty appear no
more than an aid to Orchid Cosmetics. The result had
been so good that Mark had looked dismayed, and
Brian had tried to rubbish them, until he'd realised
Mr Hedwin was delighted, whereupon he'd swiftly
changed tack.

So for the moment Delia was riding high, but her
pleasure was spoilt by the thought of what Craig
Locksley would say if he knew how she'd misrepre-
sented his thoughts.

She couldn't banish the memory of his face that
night, or the feel of his arms holding her. There'd
been no tenderness, no offer of comfort. But she'd
taken comfort, nonetheless, from the power that
seemed to flow from him. None of the other men she
knew made her feel as safe as she'd felt in those few
blinding moments. This man, who didn't bother to
hide his contempt, had shown her what was missing
in her glittering life. He'd called her lonely, and she'd
denied it. But the accusation had touched a nerve.

She'd half hoped he might contact her about
Jenny's progress, but there'd been only silence. He'd
wiped her from his mind, and the thought left an aching hollow inside her.

Mr Hedwin summoned her next morning. 'We've
hired Calloways,' he said triumphantly.

Delia said the right things. Mark's choice of advertising agency was a setback for her, but she mustn't let it show.

'I want you to see their managing director in an hour,' he went on, 'to discuss all the publicity we currently have in train. You'll find him well informed.'

Calloways had a prestigious address in the heart of London's Mayfair, in a street of elegant stone buildings. Some had been turned into shops selling exotic antiques that bore no price tags, because anyone who needed to ask couldn't afford them. There were a couple of estate agents offering apartments priced in the millions. The rest simply bore brass plates. Calloways was one of these.

A receptionist directed her to the office of the managing director. His door was slightly ajar. Delia blinked at the name on the door plate. For a moment she'd thought she'd read 'Craig Locksley'. She pulled herself together. It was time she stopped brooding on him. She was beginning to see him everywhere.

Then a cool voice that she remembered called, 'Come in, Miss Summers. I've been waiting for you.'

Dazed, Delia walked into an elegant, sun-filled office. Her worst nightmare had come true. Here was Craig Locksley, waiting for her. And now she knew that this meeting had always been inevitable. She'd been a fool to think she could escape him.

'Good morning, Mr Locksley. I'm here from Orchid Cosmetics and—and—' Her confident manner faded. 'I don't understand any of this. How can you possibly be here?'

'My partners have brilliant ideas but not a lot of business sense. I provide that.'

'I—get the picture,' she said slowly.

'No, you don't. Your ideas of blindness come out of the nineteenth century. I have a computer that talks to me, a first-rate secretary and a mind that remembers everything.'

'Everything?'

'Everything I want it to remember.'

'You didn't remember to call me about Jenny.'

'I didn't forget. I didn't think it necessary.'

'Didn't the vet tell you I kept calling him to check her progress?'

For the first time she had him at a disadvantage. 'No,' he said after a moment. 'Nobody mentioned that.'

'I was worried about her, and so glad that she was all right. Is she here with you?'

'No, she's not up to that yet.'

Craig's secretary looked in. 'Joe and Peter say they're ready when you are.'

'Then we'll be right along. They're my partners, the Calloway brothers,' he explained to Delia. 'You'll be mostly dealing with them, but I wanted to meet you first.'

'To enjoy the joke of making a fool of me?' Delia said coolly.

'No. I wanted to find out if you still struck me in the same way as last time.'

'And do I?' she couldn't help asking.

'Don't rush me. I'll tell you later.'

'Mr Locksley, I'm here professionally. We'll both

conduct our business better if we leave personal considerations out of it, and forget we ever met before.'

'You're quite right, Miss Summers. Business first and last. Let's go.' He led her confidently along the corridor to a huge, well-lit office. There were two desks, two powerful computers and a great deal of paper strewn about. He introduced her and said, 'I've got some calls to make. I'll be back later.'

The Calloway brothers were in their forties, both bald, plain and charming. Delia found them delightful, and soon realised that, as Craig had said, they were the creative brains behind the firm's brilliant advertising concepts. They cheerfully admitted that they had only the vaguest idea about money, which was why the firm had been floundering before Craig had taken it by the scruff of the neck. He'd called in debts, renegotiated loans and launched an attack on expenses that left everyone reeling.

'Including us,' Peter Calloway said, sighing. 'He's a hard taskmaster.'

'But he saved us,' Joe chimed in. 'And he keeps us safe. Can you imagine that?'

'Yes,' Delia murmured to herself. 'I can.'

'We couldn't do without him. You don't want to be fooled by his blindness. Our bank manager's terrified of him. He says that Craig always acts as though he's doing the bank a favour.'

Delia laughed, but the words 'he keeps us safe' echoed in her head. Craig Locksley presented an even greater impression of strength than he had before.

They talked for a couple of hours. The brothers were full of terrific ideas for Orchid, and Delia began to relax. They were equally complimentary about her work, especially the leaflets.

'Nice original stuff,' Peter Calloway said. 'That's why we asked your boss if we could deal with you.'

'That—was your idea, then?'

'Actually Craig suggested it. I'm not sure how he knew you'd written them, but he seems to know everything without being told. By the way, he wants you to drop in again before you go.'

She found Craig Locksley dictating letters into a machine. He stopped when she knocked.

'I've had lunch served,' he said, indicating a trolley. 'Perhaps you'd take over.'

She served up the chicken salad and crusty rolls, setting a plate beside him on the desk. He drew in a breath and seemed to be concentrating.

'Is something wrong?' Delia asked with a slight edge to her tone. 'My voice? My shoes? Do tell me.'

'Your perfume. It's wrong for you.'

'Really?' she said coolly.

'It's obviously expensive, but it doesn't suit your style.'

'I've set the coffee near your elbow,' she said. Not for the world would she have given him the satisfaction of asking what her style was.

He waited a moment, then a grin spread over his face. It had a derisive quality, as if he was calling her a coward for ducking his challenge.

'It was you who wrote those leaflets, wasn't it?' he demanded abruptly.

'Yes,' she said, trying not to sound as self-conscious as she felt.

He made a wry face. 'You didn't really understand

a word I said that night, did you? It was just grist to the cosmetics mill.'

He didn't seem angry, more disappointed, as though she'd merely confirmed his poor opinion.

'It wasn't like that,' she protested. 'I—I didn't do it cynically.'

'But you did it.'

'I had to. It's easy for you to sit there and judge—'

'I'm not judging you. I admire your shrewdness. You wasted no time going for the jugular, and that's how to get ahead.'

'It's *my* jugular that's being gone for.' Delia defended herself. 'My boss has brought his nephew into the department at the last moment, and he's trying to manoeuvre him into the top job.'

'Which, of course, cuts across your manoeuvring.'

'I've worked very hard to earn that job. Brian's trying to give Mark an easy ride, and I'm blowed if I'll let them get away with their little tricks.'

'So you tried a few little tricks of your own,' Craig said, amused. 'Well done. A display of sincerity is the cleverest trick in the book.'

Delia bit her lip. There seemed no way past his irony.

'By the way,' he added, 'I haven't quite concluded negotiations with your boss. Tell him that my final price will be ten per cent more than he's offering.'

He thrust some figures towards her. Delia stared.

'He'll never agree to that,' she said at last.

Craig grinned like a pirate about to overrun a captured vessel. 'He'll agree when he compares the quality with what he can get from Lombard's,' he said.

'We'll see.' At once Delia drew in her breath, shocked at herself. 'I'm sorry.'

'Don't be,' he snapped. 'Talk to me as though I was a normal man, because although you may not think it that's what I am.'

Before Delia could answer a young, disapproving voice from the doorway said, *'Daddy!'*

The girl from the photograph came into the office. She had an intelligent face and a cheeky smile. She had her father's dark, brilliant eyes. But, unlike his, they showed her the world. The look she gave Delia was thorough and appraising.

'Don't take any notice of Daddy,' she said cheerfully. 'He's just acting like a bear because he's lost without Jenny.'

'I'm not lost,' Craig growled.

Alison smiled at him. It was an adult smile, protective and understanding. 'No, Daddy,' she said gently.

'And don't say, "No, Daddy," like that,' he growled. 'You don't have to humour me.'

'No, Daddy.'

At last he gave a reluctant grin. 'You're a cheeky monkey.'

Alison beamed. 'Yes, Daddy.'

'Miss Summers, this is my daughter, Alison. Alison, this is Delia Summers, from Orchid Cosmetics.'

Instantly the child's face was eager. Delia guessed she was just beginning to be interested in her appearance, and found make-up an entrancing new world.

'Are you a model?' she asked, thrilled. 'I mean, do

you wear Orchid make-up so that everyone can see how terrific it is?'

'I work in the publicity department,' Delia explained.

'But they let you use everything you want?'

'Anything I want,' Delia confirmed.

Alison sighed wistfully. 'I wish I was pretty like you. I keep looking in the mirror, hoping I'll be pretty today, but it never happens.'

'But you won't discover it that way,' Delia said. 'Nobody looks pretty staring in the mirror. It's something other people see.'

'Not me,' Alison said despondently. 'My face is just wrong. Everything about it is wrong.'

'But it hasn't finished developing yet,' Delia argued. 'Wait until you're older and it'll start to look right.'

'But isn't there something I could put on it to make it right *now*?' Alison asked anxiously.

Delia couldn't resist giving Craig an impish look to see how he reacted to this heresy in his own family. Then she checked herself with a little gasp of dismay. Suddenly she felt frighteningly helpless. She had an armoury of weapons to win a man round, but they were all useless with him.

Is that all I am? she thought with horror. A collection of tricks with nothing inside?

'You don't need to put things on your face at your age,' she said quickly. 'But here—' She reached into her bag for a tiny cologne spray she always kept with her. 'Dab a little of this on behind your ears.'

'Perfume!' Alison said, thrilled.

'Not perfume,' Delia hastened to say with one eye on Craig. 'Just cologne. Use it sparingly.'

She might as well have saved her breath. Delighted with her very first cosmetic, Alison began spraying it around enthusiastically.

'Keep that away from me,' Craig said sharply. 'You shouldn't be using that muck at your age.'

Alison quietened at once, but instead of being upset at her father's unreasonable harshness, like any other child, she said quietly, 'Sorry, Daddy.' Again the hint of protectiveness was there.

He sighed. 'No, *I'm* sorry,' he said. 'I shouldn't have barked at you. Come here.'

He reached out a hand, which Alison grasped at once, and gave her a fierce hug. It was clear that she was used to coping with her father's problems. Before leaving the circle of his arms she said in a stage whisper, 'You ought to say sorry to Miss Summers too.'

'I'll be dam—what for?' he demanded. 'And don't say I'm like a bear, because I'm the most kindly man alive.'

This time Delia and Alison laughed together. To Delia's delight and surprise Craig actually looked sheepish. 'Well, maybe I'm not in the best of moods,' he conceded.

'It's not Daddy's fault,' Alison explained. 'It's because he hasn't got Jenny, his guide dog. So I have to look after him specially. But she'll be home next week, and then I'm going camping.'

'I see,' Delia said slowly, conscious that she was entering a minefield.

Alison nodded earnestly. 'She got knocked down by some stupid driver who was going too fast. Daddy

says she's the sort of woman who does everything too
fast, and causes a lot of harm, because she doesn't
think. I hate people like that, don't you?'

'Yes,' Delia said heavily. 'I do.' It took all her
courage to add, 'I'm afraid—I'm afraid the driver was
me.'

The brightness drained out of Alison's face, leaving
only puzzlement behind. 'What do you mean?' she
asked, as if unwilling to believe it.

It was even harder to say it again, but Delia forced
herself. 'I was driving the car. I hit Jenny.'

A moment ago she'd been almost a heroine to
Alison. Now the child's delight was wiped out, replaced not by anger but by shock. Delia clenched her
hands, finding that Alison's disillusionment was just
as painful as Craig's dismissiveness.

'I'm very sorry,' she said. 'I didn't mean to do it...'
Oh, the useless words, when the deed was done!

'Of course you didn't,' Alison said politely. 'It
must have been an accident. Daddy, I think I'll go
and see Uncle Joe now.'

'All right, but don't get in his way,' he said gently.

Alison spoke politely to Delia. 'Goodbye. It's been
so nice meeting you.'

No child should have to be as controlled as this,
Delia thought sadly. It would be better if she yelled
at me.

When Alison had gone she turned on Craig. 'You
could have stopped that conversation instead of letting
me walk into it,' she said angrily.

'Spare you, you mean?' he demanded. 'Why should
I? I ask no quarter and I give none.'

'Evidently. But it's a little hard on a child.'

'I didn't create that situation,' he insisted. 'I just didn't see it coming. Besides, I never expected you to admit it. That took courage.'

'I think I'll go,' Delia said. 'It was kind of you to offer me lunch, but if I stay we'll start saying unprofessional things to each other.'

'*Start* saying?'

'Good day, Mr Locksley. As you said earlier, I'll be dealing mostly with your partners, so I'm sure there won't be any need for us to meet again.'

Craig listened as her heels clicked on the marble floor of the corridor, fading into the distance. His face was expressionless. After a moment Alison returned. She went and stood quietly beside him, twining her fingers in his. He gripped her hand tensely.

'Did she really knock Jenny down?' Alison asked.

'I'm afraid so.'

'It's strange. She's not a bit the way you talked about her.'

'Why don't *you* describe her to *me*?' Craig asked.

'She's tall and slim, and ever so pretty. I mean, really pretty, not just because of the make-up. I wish my eyes were like hers—sort of big, and dark blue, with black lashes.' She sighed wistfully. 'Then I could be a siren.'

'Is that today's ambition?' he asked. 'Last week it was a vet.'

'Well, I could be a siren too.'

'Is Miss Summers a siren?'

'We-ell...' Alison considered. 'She's got a gorgeous smile.'

'Yes,' he murmured, too softly for her to hear. 'I know.'

CHAPTER FOUR

'HEY, look at that super-sexy man!'

Delia turned in smiling protest at her office junior's frank comment. But her smile died when she saw the man in Helen's sights.

Craig Locksley had just entered the reception area, with Alison. Delia was too surprised to protect herself against his impact, and the uncontrollable agitation about her heart was alarming.

'You shouldn't say things like that,' she reproved Helen. 'He might hear you.'

'But he *is* sexy,' Helen protested in a lower voice. 'Don't you think so?'

'Have you got those books I asked for? Very well, take them to my office and I'll be there in a moment.'

They were in a corridor. Delia had come looking for Helen to discover why she was taking so long, and had encountered her just where there was a good view of Reception.

Delia heard the receptionist say, 'I'll tell Mr Gorham that you're here.'

'I'm a little early for my appointment,' Craig said.

So Brian had made an appointment with Craig and had told her nothing about it, Delia mused. She was angry but not surprised. In the two weeks since her visit to Calloways Brian had several times insinuated Mark into meetings where he didn't belong, always managing to sideline Delia.

Alison waved at Delia, giving her a beaming smile. At least the child had forgiven her about Jenny, she thought with relief. She hurried forward and received an exuberant greeting.

'Good afternoon, Mr Locksley. Hello, Alison, it's nice to see you again. How's Jenny?'

'She's ever so much better, but not quite right yet,' Alison said. 'So Daddy said I could come here with him, if I promised not to pester you to let me see things, and of course I'm not going to.'

Craig was grinning, and it transformed him. 'I might have known you'd find a way around it, you little wretch,' he said.

'But honestly, Daddy, I didn't pester. I didn't even *ask*, did I, Miss Summers?'

'No, you didn't. You managed it beautifully without asking.' The three of them laughed together.

Brian appeared, full of effusive greetings. 'Craig! Wonderful! My office is this way.'

At once Alison put herself in front of her father so that he could rest his hand naturally on her shoulder. Her face was grave and concentrated as she led him to the door of Brian's office. Delia went too, but at the last moment Brian blocked her way.

'I'll send for you if I need you,' he said, flashing a brilliant, insincere smile. Delia had no choice but to step back, but not before she'd seen Mark inside the office.

'So you and I can go and look around,' she told Alison.

Delia took her first to the laboratory where new products were tested to make sure they looked and smelled right. Next they visited the salon where members of the public volunteered to be guinea pigs for Orchid's own beauty school. Delia provided Alison with a shiny bag, bearing Orchid's name and glamorous logo, and began to fill it with samples of products. She knew Craig would be annoyed if the child started painting her face, so the samples were mostly moisturisers, bath gels, talcum powders and various skin-care products. But Delia added one very pale pink lipstick in answer to a beseeching look. Then she held a finger over her lips. Alison made the same gesture, nodding in conspiracy.

Helen appeared, looking urgent. 'Mr Gorham wants you in the meeting.'

Delia handed Alison over into Helen's care and hurried to Brian's office. He smiled when she entered but she could sense a tinge of annoyance in his manner.

'Mr Locksley felt you should join us since you were the last to deal with him, although I don't really feel— However, you're here now. I understand that you knew about this proposal to increase the price. You should have told me.'

Delia gasped. 'But I did, Brian. I told you the same day, and you said—'

'I don't think so. I don't *think* so, Delia. I would have remembered that. It's very awkward being faced with something like this at the last moment.'

Delia ground her teeth to stop herself saying something very impolite. She had the feeling that Craig Locksley could follow every charged undercurrent, and was enjoying it.

'It seemed only fair to let you see what you were

paying for before we finalised the price,' he observed. 'This work is as good as you'll ever get.'

Delia went through the folder he'd brought, and was thrilled with it. The Calloway brothers had excelled themselves with a campaign that was vivid, beautiful and imaginative. Even with an extra ten per cent, they were getting full value for money.

Brian tried to hold out. 'Shall we say an extra five per cent?' he asked jovially.

'No, let's say an extra ten, because that's what it's worth,' Craig said, unruffled.

Brian turned to his nephew. 'What do you think, Mark?'

'It's excellent work,' Mark said, as if giving the matter great consideration, 'but I feel an extra five would be generous. Money's a little tight in the department at the moment—'

'Only because you wasted so much of it on Lombard's,' Craig observed. 'They raised the price twice, and you paid up, hoping they'd deliver the goods eventually. But they never did.'

'I think you've been misinformed,' Mark said defensively. 'We started from a low base with Lombard's and increased it *once*, I believe—'

'Twice,' Craig repeated, and gave the precise figures and dates. 'The details were all over town,' he added, by way of explanation. 'With Calloways you're buying the best, but the best costs.'

The haggling went on. Brian occasionally deferred to Mark, but pointedly excluded Delia. It was obvious that she was here only because Craig had insisted on it, and Brian was furious. This was a mistake. Temper was putting him at a disadvantage, while Craig coolly stood his ground. Mark yapped obediently in his uncle's wake.

'Why don't we ask your deputy for an opinion?' Craig asked at last, slightly stressing the words 'your deputy'. Delia's alert eyes caught the instinctive turn of Brian's head in Mark's direction, before he remembered that his deputy was Delia.

'I think this is superb,' she said. 'It's exactly the campaign Orchid needs.'

'Would you agree that it follows the lines discussed at your meeting with Joe and Peter?' Craig asked her.

'Perfectly. They seem to have read my mind.'

'I'll tell them you said that. They'll be flattered because they were very enthusiastic about working with you. Joe said he'd seldom met anyone who understood what she was talking about so well.'

'We're all agreed that Calloways is the best,' Brian said in a tight voice. 'That's why Mark went to such lengths to secure the firm for us. I said at the time that we could trust his instinct, and I'm glad you've come round to that point of view, Delia.'

Delia saw a faint, derisive grin on Craig's face, and knew it wasn't directed at her. He was a receiver, fine-tuned to pick up the subtlest waves, and he understood everything that was going on in this room. That was why he'd given her a boost, playing Brian and Mark at their own game.

'Well, gentleman,' he said, 'do we have a deal or not? If not, I have to be moving on.'

'We'll have to let you know,' Brian hedged.

'You can let me know right now. I have no more time to waste.'

'Look, this has been sprung on us—'

'No, Miss Summers reported my terms to you two weeks ago. You know my price. If I don't hear from you by this evening I shall conclude that the whole deal's off. Good day, gentlemen.'

Craig rose to his feet and made a slight turn. What happened next happened so fast that it was over before Delia realised what she'd done. Craig had forgotten that Jenny wasn't with him. He reached out for the dog, didn't find her, and paused, shocked and confused. Delia was close enough to tug his sleeve in the right direction without being seen by the other two. He gave no sign of recognition, but walked without further help to the door.

'Perhaps you'll be kind enough to reunite me with my daughter, Miss Summers?' he said.

'Certainly.' She managed to guide him unobtrusively until they were out of the door, then he tucked his hand into her arm.

'Thank you,' he said quietly, and she didn't have to ask what for.

She was coming to terms with her own action, with the fact that she'd instinctively taken Craig's side against the firm in helping him to leave the room with dignity. But she'd been full of admiration for the way he'd got the better of Brian and Mark.

'Alison's been doing the grand tour,' she said. 'I'll send Helen a message to bring her back. How about some coffee in the meantime?'

She guided him into her pleasant office and towards the leather sofa.

'Thank you,' he said again. 'Not just for helping me in there but for being so discreet about it. I appreciate you played it down for your own reasons, but thank you anyway.'

'What do you think my own reasons were, Mr Locksley?'

'It wouldn't have looked good if your boss had seen you giving me a gesture of support, would it?'

'No, it wasn't that,' she said quickly. 'I didn't want to see your exit ruined. I'd had so much fun watching you wipe the floor with them.'

Craig grinned, and it was the grin of an adventurer who'd brought off a risky enterprise. Delia remembered Helen saying, 'Look at that super-sexy man!' That was what you would think if you saw Craig Locksley for the first time, she realised. Not, Look at that blind man! or, Look at that helpless man! No, it would be his vibrant male attractiveness that would strike you first.

'Now I've met that pair, I forgive you for the pamphlets,' he said with a touch of unconscious arrogance. 'Uncle Brian really is determined to squeeze you out and hand the plum job to his little nephew on a plate, isn't he?'

'Exactly,' she said warmly. 'And why should I just lie down and let them get away with it? If there's a superb candidate for that job, someone better than me, I'll give in gracefully and work as their deputy. But Mark is being wormed in by intrigue.'

'And you're being nudged out by intrigue. By the way, I hope you appreciated my cunning in getting you brought in?'

'Yes, I did. Now it's my turn to thank you.' She chuckled. 'They were as mad as fire, and when you kept on about my meeting with Joe and Peter I thought Brian was going to explode.'

'How did Mark look at that moment?' Craig asked appreciatively.

'Like a little boy who'd seen a bigger boy snatch his lollipop.' They laughed together.

'You should get that job,' Craig said. 'You're more intelligent than either of them, and more responsive. You know how to take good advice.'

'Do I? How do you know?'

'I told you two weeks ago that your perfume didn't suit your style. I'm glad you took some notice. This new one is much better. It's lighter. It has a dancing quality. It's witty.'

In a moment Delia was flooded by self-consciousness. It was almost a relief that he couldn't see the blush rising to cover her face. This was ridiculous, she told herself. Why should she be as awkward as a schoolgirl because of a half-joking compliment? Yet she was completely, uncontrollably glad. In the same moment came the instinct to hide her feelings from his all-seeing inner eye.

'Actually, I was due for a change,' she said casually. 'It's my job to try out the company's products. That's all, although naturally I'm glad you like it. I'll make sure your appreciation is fed into our market research programme.'

He smiled, half to himself. 'I wonder what your market research programme would make of the thoughts going through my head at this moment?'

'Perhaps you should tell me,' she suggested lightly. Her heart had begun to beat with rapid insistence.

For a moment she thought he would answer her,

but then he said, 'Not now. Alison may arrive at any minute. Or there may be a message from your boss to say he's agreed to my terms.'

Delia felt absurdly disappointed. It made her say coolly, 'Or perhaps a message to say just the opposite.'

'No, he won't do that,' Craig said calmly. 'He can't afford to. I've got him cornered, and he knows it.'

A moment ago Delia had been in charity with him. Now she found his arrogant assurance insufferable. 'You don't suffer from a lack of confidence, do you, Mr Locksley?'

'Of course not! What would be the point?'

'What indeed?' she echoed wryly.

'While we're still alone, there's something I've been meaning to say to you. It's an apology for some of the things I said to you the night we met. I'm sorry if I went for you. Like you, I had thoughts that I couldn't erase. I needed to lash out, and you were handy.'

'Don't apologise,' she said at once. 'Who else should you lash out at but me?'

'I was angry—not entirely with you. Just—angry. I didn't expect it to hit you that way.'

'Neither did I. I'm usually so calm and collected. But then I don't usually do harm to people, or dogs.'

'I believe you,' he said quietly.

'And Jenny's really going to be all right? I thought you'd have her back by now.' To her alarm he hesitated. 'What is it? Hasn't she recovered?'

'Physically she's fine. But she was very shaken up and it's taking time for her nerves to settle down. I had a guide-dog trainer working with her for a few days. Jenny's all right indoors but she gets very unhappy if she's taken onto the road.'

'Oh, no! You mean she might never be her old self again?'

'It's possible. But she's gone back to the training centre for a while, and a few weeks there will probably put her right.'

'But suppose she's not?' Delia asked frantically. 'I never thought of anything like this. Oh, God, what have I done?'

'Delia, stop it!' Craig said firmly. 'It's too soon to panic. If there's one thing being blind has taught me it's not to anticipate trouble. Jenny will come home. I just hope it's soon. I hate having to rely on Alison.'

A thought struck Delia. 'Wasn't Alison supposed to be at camp by now?'

'Yes, she was.'

'And you kept her at home to look after you? That's monstrous!'

'Will you stop making glib judgements?' Craig demanded. 'I didn't keep her at home. I don't want her making sacrifices for me, but I couldn't force her to leave. We had a huge row about it. I laid down the law, ordered her to obey me. But I might as well have saved my breath.'

'Where's your fatherly authority?'

'It's easy to talk. My so-called fatherly authority got me precisely nowhere.'

'But that's nonsense. She's ten years old. You should simply have insisted.'

'I'd like to hear you trying to change my daughter's mind. She's as stubborn as a donkey.'

'I wonder where she gets that from.'

He gave a bark of laughter. 'OK. She gets it from me. That's how I understand her so well.'

'You could have made her go if you'd really wanted to,' Delia insisted. Her anger was out of all proportion to the situation and her feeling for Alison. Craig evidently realised this, for he turned his head in her direction, as if to catch a note in her voice more clearly. 'She'll have to be serious and responsible soon enough,' Delia said. 'Must she start now? Isn't she entitled to some freedom?'

'Certainly she is,' he said coldly. 'I'm a burden on her. I know it, and don't need reminding.'

'I didn't mean—'

'Do you think I *like* this situation, knowing that my daughter loses out on the pleasures of childhood because of me?' he demanded with a touch of bitterness. 'Listen, I can hear her voice. See if you can talk her round. You won't find it so easy.'

Alison came in, carrying her shiny bag of goodies. Her face told the story of her wonderful morning, and Delia guessed she didn't have many treats. Her overgrown sense of responsibility got in the way, and her father let it happen. She noticed how Alison gave him a quick, concerned glance before letting her youthful eagerness overflow. Well, this time, Delia thought crossly, she would force him to put his daughter first.

'I've had the most lovely time,' Alison said eagerly. 'Thank you *ever* so.'

'What have you been doing, darling?' Craig asked.

'I've been everywhere. And I've seen how they make things and—'

She bubbled on for several minutes. Many fathers would have been bored, but Delia had to give Craig full marks for listening with an appearance of interest. He even asked sensible questions.

Delia poured Alison an orange juice, and said, 'I was wondering why you weren't at camp. I know you were looking forward to it.'

'Jenny's not home yet,' Alison explained.

'But does that mean you can't go? Your father knows the way around the house—'

'And I've got an excellent secretary during the day,' Craig supplied.

'So you see,' Delia said, 'he'll be fine.'

'You don't understand,' Alison said simply. 'I can't leave Daddy alone. I just can't.'

'That's nonsense,' Craig said edgily. 'I'm a grown man and I don't need looking after.'

Alison caught Delia's eye and silently mouthed, 'He *does*.' There was a look of mulish obstinacy around her mouth that so exactly mirrored her father's that Delia almost laughed.

As if the subject were now closed Alison brought her bag over to Delia's desk and said calmly, 'Look at the lovely talcum powder they gave me.'

Then, quick as a flash, she seized a pen, scribbled something on a sheet of paper and pushed it over to Delia. It read, 'Daddy has terrible, black moods when he's alone.' Delia read it and nodded in silent comprehension.

'But why does it have to be you who stays?' she asked. 'Don't you have any family?'

'I don't need anyone,' Craig repeated.

Neither of the other two took any notice of this.

'Well, there's Grandma and Grandpa—my mother's parents,' Alison explained. 'But it can't be them because Grandma changes everything around in the kitchen, and she drives Daddy mad fussing. And Grandpa tells the same fishing stories over and over.'

'That would be unbearable even for a man who could see,' Delia agreed sympathetically.

'It would be unbearable even for a man who was interested in fishing,' Craig growled. 'Which I'm not. How many times do I have to say that I'll be fine on my own? Alison, you will get yourself off to camp, and that's an order.'

'Daddy, we've been through all this,' Alison said in an uncannily adult voice. 'I thought I'd made it plain.'

'Yes, you did, and now *I'm* making myself plain. I'm calling the camp to say you'll be there this evening.'

This time Alison said nothing, but simply sat with her hands folded and the stubborn look about her mouth again. Evidently Craig could interpret the silence because he said furiously, 'And don't sit there looking at me like that.'

'Like what, Daddy?'

'Like you are doing. Do you think I can't hear the expression on your face?'

'No, Daddy, I know you can. That's why I don't need to say I'm not going.'

'Thus demolishing my reputation with Miss Summers. She thinks this is all my fault.' He glared at Delia. 'Well, I hope you know better now.'

Afterwards she wasn't sure if she'd already made her decision, or was still inching towards it, but something made her say, 'OK, there's a problem. But there's also a solution.'

'Then you tell us what it is,' Craig said.

'All right, I will. I'll stay with you.'

'You?' His astonishment was unflattering but Delia refused to be disconcerted.

'Yes, me. I won't change things round, or talk too much, or fuss. I'll be like Jenny, just *being* there.' She appealed to Alison. 'How does that sound?'

'That would be wonderful!' Alison breathed. 'I know Daddy would be all right with you, and then I could go to camp. Oh, thank you, *thank you.*'

Craig's protest died on his lips. Alison's joy had got through to him, and there was no way he could spoil it for her now. Delia read everything in his face.

'You won't find me so bad,' she said lightly. 'I'll stay out of your way and not speak unless I'm spoken to.'

Alison giggled and smothered it quickly.

'You find something funny?' Craig growled.

'No, Daddy, honestly.' The child composed her features.

'You haven't left me much choice between you,' he said.

'Does that mean you say yes?' Alison pleaded.

'If I do, will you go to camp?'

'Oh, *yes.*'

'Then I agree. Thank you, Miss Summers.' His tone was polite but Delia felt the words were wrenched out of him.

'Where is the camp?' she asked.

He told her. It was only about twenty miles away.

'I'll drive her down this evening as soon as I finish work,' Delia offered, but then saw Alison shaking her head vigorously, and raised her eyebrows in a silent question.

'Can you come home first so that I can show you your room?' Alison asked. Then she mouthed, 'And explain things.'

'You're giving Miss Summers a great deal of trouble—' Craig began, but Delia interrupted him quickly.

'I think it's much better if I come home first. Now, why don't you call the camp and tell them Alison will be there today?'

He did so while Alison danced about the room, singing, 'I'm going to camp, I'm going to camp.'

Delia's internal phone rang. It was Brian. 'Is Locksley still here?' he demanded.

'Yes, he's with me now.'

'Then bring him back to my office. We're going to have to pay his price. It's too late to negotiate. It's a pity you didn't tell me about it earlier.'

'I *did* tell you—' she began to say furiously. But Brian had hung up.

'Will you please return to Mr Gorham's office?' she said. 'He's going to pay your price.'

'Of course.'

'People always do what Daddy wants,' Alison said cheekily.

'That's rich, coming from you,' Craig informed her with a grin. 'Miss Summers, just give me a few minutes, and we'll go straight home so that you can pack.'

'I'll come as soon as I've finished work,' she promised.

CHAPTER FIVE

ALISON was waiting at the window as Delia drove up. The next moment she was pulling the door open and eagerly taking her by the hand to lead her straight upstairs.

She'd given Delia a corner room that was sunny and pleasant, with plenty of space. She watched as Delia unpacked, oohing and aahing over her clothes.

Craig greeted her briefly then returned to his computer while Alison showed her the secrets of the kitchen, and stressed again the importance of never moving anything by so much as a quarter of an inch.

'You won't actually have to do any housework,' she explained like a solemn little professor. 'Mrs Gage does that. She comes in to clean every day, except weekends. The car collects Daddy each morning and brings him home in the evening. During the day his secretary, Alexandra, looks after him, and he gets home at about seven.'

'And that's when I've got to be here?'

Alison nodded. 'He can do all the practical things for himself,' she said in a lowered voice, 'but when he's on his own he minds terribly about being blind. You see, he wasn't always blind. He can remember how things should look and he—well, he just *minds*. When he's going through a bad time I've seen him put his arms round Jenny and hug her ever so tight. But it's all right,' she added as if a thought had struck

68

her. 'You don't have to hug Daddy. Just talk to him, and let him hear you moving about.'

She gave Delia a list that had obviously been prepared with care. It concerned Craig's habits, the fact that he rose early and went to bed late, and didn't like talking at the table. Delia read it thoroughly.

'What are you two whispering about?' Craig demanded, appearing in the kitchen doorway.

'Nothing, Daddy. I was just telling Miss Summers where to find things. Oh, yes, and coffee.' She turned back to Delia. 'Daddy likes it very strong—'

'That's enough,' Craig snapped. 'For heaven's sake stop mother-henning me. I don't need all this fuss.'

There was a silence, during which Alison's eyes were suspiciously bright. Then she said, 'I'll get my things,' and rushed past her father.

'That was a rotten thing to do,' Delia said furiously. 'You made her cry. Why can't you accept her help graciously?'

'Because I don't want anyone's help,' he said savagely, and turned away.

Alison reappeared with her suitcase, having regained her composure. 'We're off now,' she said brightly. 'Goodbye, Daddy.'

'Aren't I allowed to come in the car with you?'

'Are you sure you're not too busy?' she said wistfully.

Craig touched her cheek. 'I'm never too busy for you, chicken,' he said. 'Besides, I expect you've got a load of last-minute instructions to give me.'

He sat with her in the back seat, holding her hand and listening meekly while Alison lectured him about safety precautions. Delia had to admit that when Craig did something he did it properly. He was trying to atone for his bear-like behaviour, and was obviously succeeding. Alison's tears were forgotten and she was as happy as a lark.

They arrived just after eight o'clock. There was still a warm sun by which to see the white-painted wooden huts set under the trees. Everywhere there were girls of Alison's age. Some of them bounced over to them, greeting her eagerly. They were followed by the camp superintendent, a pleasant, middle-aged woman who calmed the riot and introduced herself as Miss Jeffries.

'I'm so glad Alison was able to join us, Mr Locksley,' she said. 'If you'll both come to my office we can have a cup of tea and complete the formalities.'

Delia waited for Alison to take Craig's arm, but instead the child stood back, watching her. She understood. Alison wanted to see her perform her duties, so that she would know her father was in safe hands. Delia guided Craig's hand so that he could clasp her arm.

She concentrated all her mental energy on anticipating his needs, but he knew how to manage better than she did. As they approached the hut that did duty as an office she murmured, 'Here we are,' and felt his fingers tighten on her arm. To her relief he climbed the three steps with confidence.

Inside, Miss Jeffries indicated a couple of chairs. Delia said, 'Why don't you sit *here*?' scraping the chair slightly against the floor so that the noise would direct him.

'There are a couple of papers for you to sign, giving

Alison into our care,' Miss Jeffries explained. 'Who will sign?'

'I will,' Craig said immediately.

Delia put the pen in his hand, and guided his fingers to the space. To her relief he wrote his name firmly. Alison looked cheerful, as if a weight had been lifted off her mind.

Craig said goodbye to his daughter, and stayed where he was while Delia went to Alison's hut and saw her exchanging eager greetings with other girls. When she was satisfied, she left.

As she drove home he said, 'Thank you. You managed it beautifully.'

'Alison was watching,' Delia told him. 'One false step from me and she'd have insisted on coming back.'

'She really wanted to go to that camp, didn't she? Much more than I realised.'

'She's a little girl. It's natural that she wants to be with other children. It's a lovely camp. I saw tennis courts and a swimming pool.'

'You sound as if you'd like to be there yourself,' he said with a grin.

'Of course not. I just think it's nice for her.'

'No, there was a longing note in your voice.' When she didn't answer he said, 'What is it? Did I hit a nerve?'

'Well, maybe I was thinking of a trip I missed when I was a child,' she admitted reluctantly.

'Is that why you got so defensive on Alison's behalf?'

'Perhaps.'

'Tell me about it.'

'Goodness, there's nothing to tell,' she said lightly. 'It's too trivial to talk about.'

To her relief he didn't press the subject, and for the rest of the journey they talked about inconsequential things.

Delia didn't make the mistake of trying to guide him when they reached home. As before, he managed the steps easily and put his key in the lock.

'I could do with a coffee,' she suggested.

'Then I'll make you one. After that we have things to talk about.'

'Don't worry,' she said as he moved around the kitchen. 'I promise not to get in your way.'

'That's not exactly—' He broke off as the telephone rang, and picked up the receiver on the kitchen wall. 'Hello, darling.'

So it was Alison. Delia watched as Craig's smile grew tense.

'Of course I got home safely. Miss Summers is a very good driver...yes, she's here.' He held out the receiver. 'She wants to talk to you.'

Alison sounded full of relief when she heard Delia. 'I just wanted to make sure everything was all right.'

'Everything's fine,' Delia assured her. 'You get on with your holiday, and enjoy yourself.'

At last the little girl was reassured. Delia passed her back to her father, then rescued the coffee which was about to perk.

'Did I make it right?' she asked as Craig sipped it. 'Very strong.'

'It's perfect,' he said in a tight voice, 'but I think I should make it plain that the farce stops here.'

'I beg your pardon?'

'I pretended to fall in with this outrageous idea because otherwise Alison wouldn't have gone. But I never had any intention of carrying it through, and now she's safely at the camp, I want you to leave.'

'But I can't!' Delia said, angry and astonished. 'I promised her—'

'Miss Summers, I'm trying to keep my temper, because I'm very aware of what you did for my daughter, and believe me I'm grateful. But if you think the two of us can share a roof then you must be out of your mind. I may be blind, but I can't stand being treated as a cripple at the best of times—and with you of all people!'

Delia set down her cup sharply. 'Mr. Locksley, let me make my position plain. I'm not doing this for you, but for Alison, who's getting a rough deal. Left to myself I'd rather jump off a cliff than spend one moment with a man who has all the charm and graciousness of a wire-wool scraper. As for being under the same roof, if there were ten thousand other people under the same roof I would still feel your presence as an irritant.'

'That being the case, you'll have no difficulty in doing as I wish and departing.'

'But what about Alison? If she telephones she'll expect to find me here.'

'She just did, and you *were* here. She won't call again tonight because Miss Jeffries will insist she goes to bed.'

'And tomorrow night?'

'I'll work late and call her from the office. Don't worry, I'll find ways to cover your absence.'

'At least let me drop in here for an hour on my way home—'

'No,' he said fiercely. 'Don't you understand? *No*.'

'If you put it that way, no, I don't understand. It's beyond me how any man can be so pigheaded and self-righteous, and so *emotionally* blind. You pride yourself that your inner eye can see things that the rest of us miss. But you've never tried to see things from Alison's perspective. If you had, you'd show her a little more patience and kindness. But you can only think of what it's like for you. And being physically blind is no excuse for that.'

She ran upstairs and began to pack her clothes in a fury. She wasn't only angry with him but with herself too. She'd genuinely made her offer for Alison's sake, but now she could see that the thought of spending some time with him had appealed to her. In their enforced closeness she might have found something she was seeking. She couldn't put a name to it, but her instincts told her the answer lay with this difficult man. But in the light of his cruel rejection her thoughts seemed like ridiculous, schoolgirl dreams.

Normally she was a meticulous packer, taking care of her things. But now she shoved them in anyhow and slammed the case shut, longing to get away from here.

Craig was standing in the hall as she went down. She departed without speaking to him. She was afraid that her voice might betray her emotion. Besides, what was there to say?

Back in her own flat, in her own bed, Delia was just nodding off to sleep when the phone by her bed rang.

It was Craig, sounding uncharacteristically hesitant. 'I'm sorry if I woke you.'

'Not really. What's wrong?'

'Alison called a few minutes ago.'

Delia sat up in bed. 'But it's nearly eleven o'clock. You said they wouldn't let her call again.'

'Apparently it's camp policy never to prevent a child calling home, at any time of the night or day. She was worried that you weren't here. I told her you'd gone home to fetch something you'd forgotten. But—' he seemed to be having difficulty with the words '—she's calling back in an hour. If you're not here she's quite capable of returning tomorrow.' There was a silence, in which Delia was almost sure she could hear the sound of Craig grinding his teeth. 'I know you think I behaved unforgivably—'

'Think?'

'All right. I did behave unforgivably, but for Alison's sake I'm asking you to return.'

'For how long? Just long enough to fool her? Because I won't be part of that.'

'No, it wouldn't work. I see that now.'

'The original deal?'

'The original deal.'

'And you'll stick to it as you promised?'

This time she was sure he ground his teeth. 'I'll stick to it,' he said, sounding desperate. 'Will you come back, *please*?'

'Yes, I will. For Alison's sake we'll just have to put up with each other.'

A few minutes later, dressed and repacked, Delia emerged from her room. Maggie, the friend who was staying with her for a few weeks, called from the kitchen, 'Come and have some tea before you go.'

Delia gratefully accepted a cup. 'How did you know I was going?'

'Elementary, my dear Watson. I was eavesdropping. He's really got under your skin, hasn't he?'

'I'm doing it for his daughter,' Delia explained, a trifle stiffly.

'Sure you are.' Maggie eyed her spooning sugar into her cup. 'I think I hate you most when you do that,' she said affably. 'It never puts so much as an ounce on you. Why can't you get fat like the rest of us? Or at least spotty.'

'It's a pity I can't,' Delia mused. 'That might make him approve of me.'

'I thought you didn't care about his opinion.'

'I don't,' Delia said firmly.

Craig was obviously listening for her because he opened the door as she drew up. By the time she was out of the car he'd descended the steps. 'Let me take your case,' he said.

'I can manage.'

'Delia, it's my eyes that are useless, not my arms. Give me your case.'

She set it down by his feet. He carried it all the way to her room without missing a step, and she followed. Once there he seemed awkward. 'It was good of you to come back,' he said politely. 'I assure you I appreciate it.'

Delia gazed at him in dismay. 'This will be impossible if you're going to talk to me like that,' she said.

'Like what?'

'Like *that*! It's awful.'

'I thought I was perfectly polite.'

'You were. That's what I can't stand. It doesn't sound like you. I preferred you growling at me. After all, I can always growl back. But if you're going in for frigid courtesy I'm out of here.'

Craig gave a reluctant grin. 'Am I as bad as that?'

'Dreadful,' she said frankly. 'But that's all right. I can cope with dreadful. It's when you start trying to say the right thing I get confused.'

'It's going to be a great few days,' he agreed wryly.

'It's gone midnight,' Delia said. 'I can't believe Alison is really going to call now, so I—there's the phone!'

'Answer it quickly.'

She hurried down and snatched up the phone. 'Hello?'

'It's really you,' Alison said eagerly. 'I thought—well, you know—that you might not be there.'

'Of course I'm here,' Delia said brightly. 'I promised, didn't I?' The sight of Craig coming into the room made her add, 'Daddy promised too, and you know he always keeps his word.' Craig made a wry face in her direction. 'But you shouldn't be out of bed at this time.'

'I'll go back to bed now. Honestly. Are you all right, settled in and everything?'

'I'm really comfortable. You did a great job.'

'What did you forget?'

'What?'

'Daddy said you went home for something you'd forgotten.'

'Oh, that.' Delia collected her wits frantically.

'There was another suitcase with a special dress I need to wear tomorrow.'

'Daddy didn't seem to know what it was.'

'Of course not. He's a man. What do they know?'

Alison gave a conspiratorial giggle. 'Is he standing there glaring at you?'

'He certainly is.'

'Can I talk to him?'

She handed the receiver to Craig and listened while he bid his daughter goodnight. At last he hung up and said, 'I think we convinced her. Thank you. I don't know what I'd have done if you'd refused to help me.'

'I never would have refused.'

'No, you play fair. I'll give you that.'

'I'd like to make myself some tea.'

'I'll make it.'

'There's no need. You don't have to prove to me—'

'I'm not. I just don't want you blundering about in my kitchen until you've learned where everything goes. If you put things down in the wrong place, I'm lost.'

'I know. Alison told me, and you snarled at her for it.'

'OK, I give in. You make it.'

She made tea carefully, replacing everything in its exact place. When she'd finished he felt around the pots and gave a grunt of approval.

'Do I get top marks?' she asked.

'We-ll, you put the squirrel back a quarter of an inch out.'

'I *what*?'

He grinned. 'Only joking. Well done. I'll let you pour.'

As she did so he explained, 'I have groceries delivered, always the same. We stocked up this afternoon, and Alison put everything in its right place, so you won't have to worry about that. Are you hungry?'

'I've just realised that I am.'

He put two slices of bread into the toaster. While they waited she said, 'Perhaps you'd better explain my duties to me.'

'You mean Alison hasn't?' he asked with a smile.

'She said a car collects you in the mornings and brings you back.'

'That's right. There's no need for you to hurry back, as long as you're here when Alison calls.'

'Alison will call early, to make sure I'm not cutting corners,' Delia mused. 'And she'll call again, late, to make sure I haven't gone out and left you alone.'

'I'm afraid you're right. It's going to be pretty much a prison sentence for you.'

'I'll manage, as long as you don't bite my head off too often.'

As he buttered the toast he asked, 'And what will it do for your career to be leaving work on the dot every night? Don't kid yourself that Mark won't notice and make capital out of it.'

'You let me worry about Mark. I've said I'll do this and I will.'

His expression became gentler. 'You're doing all this for my daughter?'

And for you, she thought. To spend time with you, and see your face soften towards me like that. Maybe you'll get to like me, and smile at me sometimes. I know I'm taking a risk, but something is happening to me that's never happened before. It makes me nervous, but I have to go forward.

'What is it?' he asked suddenly. 'What are you thinking?'

'I—nothing. This toast is very good.'

'You wouldn't tense up like that because of the toast. The air was jagged. You were having thoughts you couldn't tell me.'

To her dismay Delia felt herself blushing furiously. Could he discern that too?

'I have a lot of thoughts that I can't tell you, because they're not your business,' she said firmly. 'And I resent being interrogated.'

'Just as long as you and Alison aren't cooking something up that I don't know about.'

She relaxed. He wasn't on the right track after all.

The phone rang. 'I don't believe it,' Craig said. 'It can't be that little imp again.' He snatched the phone up. 'Yes?' Then a black scowl came over his face. He rapped out, 'Yes, she's here.' He handed the receiver to Delia. 'A man for you.'

'Hello?'

'So there you are,' came a familiar voice.

'*Laurence?* Whatever are you doing, calling me at this hour?'

'I tried your apartment and your friend told me what you were up to.'

'Can I just—?'

'Are you raving mad?' he interrupted her. 'If ever there was a time when you needed to give all your attention to your work this is it. And what are you doing? Playing Florence Nightingale.'

CHAPTER SIX

THE next evening was enlivened by a visit from Craig's sister, Grace. She was a robust, outspoken woman with a grating voice, but a no-nonsense attitude that Delia found appealing.

'Heaven help you!' she declared when she got Delia on her own. 'Being shut up with my brother is my idea of hell. Of course I should have offered to do it myself, but my boss is sending me abroad tomorrow.' Grace was a high-ranking civil servant attached to the diplomatic corps.

'Actually there's another reason,' she confided. 'Craig can't stand having me around. Says it makes him want to chuck things.'

'That's not very nice of him,' Delia said, aghast.

'Don't worry,' Grace hooted cheerfully. 'He has the same effect on me. Anyway, he's never very nice, as I expect you've already discovered.'

'He's certainly not sweetness and light.'

'Well, to be fair to him, he was a lot better before he went blind. Are you making coffee? Fine. I like mine strong.' She closed the kitchen door and settled herself at the table.

'How long has he been blind?' Delia asked.

'Only about seven years. It hit him terribly hard because he'd always been a high achiever. It was expected in our family. If you didn't come first it meant you just weren't trying. He was a businessman, a fi-

nancial wizard, and an athlete on the side. On the day
he married Philippa he seemed to have everything a
man could want. He was crazy about her, and she was
considered quite a catch. She turned out to be a cold-
hearted little schemer, but she had great looks. Not as
brilliant as yours, but enough to knock their eyes out.'

'How did he lose his sight?'

'Hurt himself in the gym. Fell off the parallel bars
and landed on his head. When he woke up, he was
blind.'

'How terrible!'

'For a while it destroyed him. He went into a black
depression. At first they weren't sure it was perma-
nent, and Philippa played the loyal wife to perfection.
''We'll fight this together, darling,'' and so forth. But
when she realised that this was how it would always
be she changed her tune. She didn't fancy being
shackled to a blind man. I think she married him for
money and an exciting life, and suddenly the money
dried up and it wasn't exciting any more. She left him
for a man called Frank Elward, taking Alison.

'Oddly enough, that was the thing that jerked Craig
back to life. He knew Elward was a nasty bit of goods,
with criminal friends. Craig said he wasn't going to
let his daughter be raised in that atmosphere, and he
took them to court. Of course, Philippa used his blindness against him, said he couldn't cope with a child.
But Craig was armed with some very unpleasant information about Elward. And he won.

'He even offered to take Philippa back, rather than
part her from Alison. But for all Philippa's prattle
about loving her baby she chose Elward. After that
Craig really got going. He learned Braille, got a guide

dog, which he'd refused before. He studied every technique for overcoming the obstacle of his blindness. Then he went out and conquered the world again.'

'I'm glad you told me all this,' Delia said slowly. 'Now I know why he seems to be fighting all the time.'

'He is. And he can't win, because at heart he wants to believe that he isn't blind. He almost defeats it, but he can't come to terms with it, and he's filled with anger and frustration.'

The next moment she put a finger to her lips. She'd heard Craig's footsteps outside.

'I hope you're not talking about what I think you are,' he growled, opening the door.

'You mean you?' Grace asked robustly. 'Forget it. Why should anyone want to talk about you?'

'If you're telling Delia that I'm a monster of tyranny and ingratitude, you needn't bother. She's already discovered that.'

Though brother and sister had scarcely a good word to say to each other Delia noticed that they hugged each other with real affection when Grace left. She left with a wave, saying, 'Goodbye, Delia. I hope you're still alive at the end of your ordeal.'

'Be off with you,' Craig called, grinning.

After a few days Delia found she'd slipped into Craig's routine easily. They were polite to each other at breakfast, except for a tense moment one morning when she carelessly left the coffee in the wrong place. But she soon learned where everything went, and made no more mistakes.

She would reach his home in the evenings to find that he'd already started to prepare supper. She suspected that he did this deliberately, to underline his independence, and was sure of it when he asked her opinion of the food with a sardonic expression. She was able to praise it honestly. He was an excellent cook. Delia came to understand that in this, as in everything else, he felt the need to excel.

Alison always called soon after supper, and for her sake they would sound cheerful and friendly. The child was having a wonderful time, and Delia was glad of whatever instinct had prompted her to take on the care of this prickly man.

There were times when Craig seemed barely to know she was there, which was disconcerting to a woman used to the attention of men. If she could have known how hard it was for him to assume an indifferent front her heart might have been lighter.

For Craig her presence was as much of a strain as he'd feared. Every fibre of him was aware of her. With the super-developed senses of the blind man he knew each tiny movement she made. If they were in the same room he would hear her soft breathing, and know exactly how far away from him she was. Her light movements told him of her gracefulness. He would try not to picture it, try not to imagine her slim, elegant body, because that way lay madness. But he couldn't shut down his imagination, which loved to dwell on her.

Often her perfume would reach him. It was usually the one he'd told her he liked, but always something light and flowery. Occasionally she wore no perfume at all, and that was almost worse, because then he had the scent of *her*, warm, womanly, elusive.

He'd once been glad not to have been born blind, because at least he could remember how things looked. But now he felt it would almost be better not to know about the beauty of a woman, to have no way of picturing her. He might have suffered less. But to be always in the presence of loveliness, to know its separate components without seeing how they made one perfect whole—this was torture. The darkness had never been so terrible.

The more he felt her presence as a desirable woman, the more conscious he was of his blighted condition. He'd feared this and tried to send her away. It had been almost a relief when Alison had forced him to bring her back. But the relief had been short-lived. Laurence had called. Laurence, the boyfriend. There was bound to be one, of course, and he could only be grateful to have learned about him at the start.

He could still hear her voice that first night, low and urgent. 'I can't talk now...I'll call you from work in the morning...please, Laurence, don't call me here.'

Pity, he thought with loathing. Be kind to the blind man from on high, and feel good about it. Real life is somewhere else. At one time...

He wouldn't let himself think about the past, when he'd been a whole man, and could have made her want him. He would go insane if he thought about that.

One evening Delia came home to find no evidence of Craig. Usually he was in the kitchen, and would sing out to her that coffee was ready and dinner was coming up soon. But tonight there was no sign of him. She'd just decided that he would be home late when she heard an unusual sound from the rear of the house. It consisted of creaking, thumping, and someone breathing heavily. Worried in case he'd injured himself, she hurried through to a back room she'd never seen before, and opened the door. Then she stopped on the threshold, thunderstruck by the sight that met her eyes.

It was a wide, sunny room, equipped as a gymnasium. Everything was here: weights, machines and more traditional equipment—a vaulting horse, parallel bars, climbing ropes. And there, working on the parallel bars, was Craig.

He was almost naked, covered only in a pair of black, very brief briefs. They were made of some shiny material, and clung to him damply, hiding almost nothing. Craig's whole body glistened from the vigour of his workout. Delia had always guessed that he was athletically built, but now she saw it for herself. His shoulders were broad and powerful, the arms muscular. There wasn't an ounce of fat on him, from his smooth chest to his flat stomach and lean hips. Everywhere was taut and full of force.

Craig was so absorbed in what he was doing that he hadn't heard her enter. Delia knew she shouldn't watch him while he was unaware. But admiration held her rooted to the spot. His movements were smooth and confident as he placed his hands with practised ease in the right places on the bars, swinging back and forth swiftly and gracefully.

She held her breath as he whirled, somersaulting off the bars and returning to them with his body facing the opposite direction. His face was fierce with concentration, and she guessed it was no accident that he'd chosen the equipment from which he'd had his fall. The bars were an enemy that had injured him, and now he had to prove himself their master.

He twisted, swung, did handstands. The light from the windows caught every bead of perspiration, bathing him in a golden glow. He was beautiful, she thought. Not just handsome, but beautiful in a magnificent way. Every line of him spoke of authority. Many of his moves would have been dangerous in less assured hands, but he never faltered.

As Delia's gaze was fixed on the broad, powerful shoulders, the thighs thick with muscles, she suddenly found her mind possessed by shameless, wanton thoughts. She blushed at the images that were conjured up as he twisted and turned. She'd thought of herself as cool and level-headed where men were concerned. She knew that she inspired their sensual fantasies, but no man had ever sent her own thoughts rioting. Until this moment.

Now there seemed no way of controlling the brazen ideas that chased through her head. The blush seemed to be spreading from her face throughout her whole body, so that she felt hot all over, and every inch of her was alive to him.

He began to go faster, trying things which made her want to cry out a warning. But she kept quiet. He would never forgive her if he knew she'd watched him. As he made his final somersault off the bars she backed quietly out of the room and closed the door.

She went straight to the kitchen and tried to think of mundane things, but he was there with her, in her consciousness, overpowering her with his presence, filling her with a yearning need that made thought impossible. She took a deep breath and sat down abruptly. Her hands were shaking. So was the rest of her.

'I've got to pull myself together,' she said firmly. 'This is nonsense. Where's the recipe book? I'll try something new.'

But the words swam together. Delia tried harder to concentrate.

Craig came into the kitchen half an hour later, fully dressed.

'I'm making supper tonight,' she told him. 'I'm trying out a brand-new recipe, so be warned.'

'Fine.' He gave her a smile. His workout had left him in a good mood.

'I thought you were out,' Delia said. 'There was no sign of you when I came in. Have you been busy?'

'Working in my room,' he said quickly. 'I've got a big meeting the day after tomorrow. Alex, my secretary, should be calling.'

Delia made some suitable reply. Her thoughts were out of control again. They persisted in looking through his clothes at the nearly naked magnificence she'd seen in the gym.

'What book are you taking the recipe from?' he asked. 'No, don't tell me. Let's see if I can find out.'

He ran light fingers along the spine and outer edge of the book. 'It feels like one of my old ones,' he said cheerfully. 'I used it to teach Alison. She read it out and I explained what— Hang on! Why are you reading it upside down?'

'I'm not,' she said frantically.

'Yes, you are. There's a tear in the cover, just here. I know the shape. But it's at the bottom.' He gave a hilarious grin. 'How come you didn't even notice it was upside down?'

'I—I was daydreaming,' she said. 'I've—got a lot on my mind.'

'Delia,' he said, puzzled, 'you sound half-witted.' His eyes gleamed with humour and he grasped her shoulders firmly. His sudden touch, the nearness of his face were so unnerving in the midst of her turbulent thoughts that she jumped.

'What's the matter?' he asked in a gentler voice. 'You're shaking. Did I startle you?'

'Yes—yes, you did,' she gabbled.

'This isn't like the cool, efficient Miss Summers.'

'I'm not always cool and efficient,' she protested. 'Sometimes—my thoughts just get—carried away.'

To her intense relief he let her go. 'I can see supper's going to be very interesting. Perhaps I should take a stomach powder first.'

'Forget new recipes,' she said briskly. 'It's going to be ham and eggs.'

'Fine by me.' He left the kitchen, chuckling. Delia breathed out hard. Then a slow smile spread over her face at the sound of his laughter. It was a good sound.

Over supper he teased her some more, but she'd recovered her poise and gave as good as she got. It was a merry meal. He even managed to laugh when he spilt his coffee over himself.

While he was upstairs changing, the phone rang. Delia answered it, expecting to hear Alison. 'Hello?'

'Craig, please.' The young woman on the other end sounded slightly superior.

'I'm afraid he's not here. Can I help? Or can I get him to call you back?'

'This is Alexandra Mason, his personal assistant. I'm in the north, doing a report for Craig. I've called to say that it'll take longer than I thought and I won't be back until Friday.'

'Does he know where to call you?' Delia asked.

Miss Mason named a hotel, but added, 'I have to go out at once, so he may miss me.'

When Craig appeared Delia said, 'Your personal assistant called.'

'I don't have one.'

'Alexandra Mason.'

He grinned. 'Oh, I see. Alex is my secretary. She keeps hinting to be called personal assistant because she thinks it sounds more important, but so far I've turned a deaf ear. She's very efficient, but she's only been with me a short time, and there's something about her I'm still not quite sure of. What did she want?'

'To say she can't get back until Friday. The report you asked for is taking longer than expected.'

His grin faded. 'Damn! I knew it might take an extra day, but not that long.'

'I've got the number of her hotel, but she said she was going straight out.'

She read him the number and he dialled it, but sure enough Alexandra was missing.

'Can you manage without her that long?' Delia asked.

'I can get one of the other secretaries—there are several that I've used before, for routine work. But the day after tomorrow I'm going to a shareholders' meeting of—' He named a company that had been much in the news for its complacent management and highly paid board. 'I'm going to make life very uncomfortable for some fat-cat directors who want to award themselves huge pay rises. That's where I really needed her. She knows the figures and the background. I can't take a clerk from the office pool for that. It wouldn't be fair.'

Delia thought quickly. She had some leave due to her. 'I'll do it,' she said.

'You?' His emphasis wasn't flattering.

'Why not? I'm really quite bright, whatever you think.'

'I'm sure you are, but it wouldn't be easy to take this over at the last minute. I'm very demanding—'

'No, really?'

He grinned. 'You've no idea how bad I can be. It's tough. You need to be on the ball the whole time.'

'And you don't think a bimbo like me can manage it? Thanks.'

'Delia, I'm not trying to be insulting—'

'No, just managing it without trying,' she said lightly.

'It's the day after tomorrow. You'd have to take time off work.'

'Then I'll take it. I'm due for some leave. You don't want to miss your meeting, do you?'

'No, I damn well don't. But what about the dreaded Mark?'

'Even the dreaded Mark can hardly do much in one day. I'll be there. Just brief me.'

'Fine. In that case, let's start now.'

Under his direction she called up certain files on his computer.

'These figures show that the firm has made huge profits recently,' he explained, 'but at a dreadful cost. They're predators, buying up smaller firms, closing them down and throwing out the employees. But they still manage to produce the goods. And how? Because they import them cheaply from countries which use child slave labour.'

'But that's wicked,' Delia exploded.

'Yes, it is. What's more, the chairman who's been responsible for this is about to retire and award himself a bonus of a million. He ought to be in gaol, not wallowing in money.'

'Can the shareholders stop it?'

'In theory, yes. In practice it's going to be very hard. The big institutions who own shares will vote with the board, because the members of their boards are all planning the same thing. You scratch my back, I'll scratch yours. The small shareholders find it hard to make an impact because they're not organised, and they haven't got a voice.'

'And you're going to be the voice?'

'I've been writing round to as many as I can, and if they're given a strong lead it may be enough to block this proposal, and get the whole nasty business out in the open. But we need everything at our fingertips. Suppose I ask you for the up-to-date facts about—' He named an aspect of the company's work. 'Which file would you call up?'

After a moment's thought she got it right. She got the next one even faster. The third one she made a mess of.

'No,' he said irritably. 'You'll have to do better than that. I don't want you making me look an idiot in there. Perhaps we'd better forget the whole idea.'

'We will not,' Delia said firmly. 'I'll get it right.'

They worked for three hours. At the end of it her head was aching but she was exhilarated because she'd mastered the problem. Even Craig had to admit, 'You're getting it. Not bad at all.' Which she took to be praise of a high order.

'OK, just transfer those files onto the laptop, make sure it has fresh batteries, and we're in business. And don't glare at me like that.'

'I won't ask how you know.'

He smiled wryly. 'It was written all over the air. Hate! Hate!'

'Not hate,' she protested. 'Actually I rather enjoyed it, even though you *are* the world's worst tyrant.'

'You call *that* tyranny? You've seen nothing yet.'

She threw up her hands, crying, 'I believe it. I believe it.' They laughed together.

Next day she made sure that all her work was up to date, left Helen properly briefed, and cleared it with Brian for her to take a day off.

'That's fine,' he said genially. 'You've been working very hard. I expect you feel the need of a nice restful day.'

'I get the feeling that restful is the last thing it's going to be,' Delia said cheerfully.

In this she was proved right. Craig insisted on leaving very early the next morning, to be there before the rush for seats. The meeting was to be held in a cinema.

'It was the only place they could find big enough,'

Craig confided as she drove through the London traffic. 'The original venue was much smaller, but then
they got all these acceptances, and had to revise their
plans.'

'Because of you?'

'Let's say that it was after I contacted the other
shareholders that the cinema was booked.' Whatever
he might say, his whole being radiated confidence in
his own effectiveness.

Because they were early Delia managed to park the
car close to the cinema. They walked the short distance back and were almost the first waiting for the
doors to open. After that the queue lengthened rap-
idly.

'A lot of people have turned up,' she told him.

'Good. The more the merrier. I'll give those swine
a run for their money.'

He would, too, she thought. There was a fierce light
in his blind eyes. This was a man to be reckoned with,
even perhaps to be feared. There would be no pris-
oners taken today.

At last the outer doors opened. Craig tucked his
arm into Delia's.

'Smooth tiled floor, no steps,' she said. 'The door
to the auditorium is about twenty feet away.' He
stepped forward with apparent ease until they neared
the door.

Here they encountered a problem Delia hadn't anticipated. It was a shareholders-only meeting, and she
had no shares.

'Sorry, no journalists,' the steward said firmly.

'I'm not a journalist,' Delia said.

'Hmm. How do I know that? The press isn't allowed in this meeting, but your lot will try anything.'

'She's my eyes,' Craig said. He explained his blindness and his need of her in a quiet, almost meek voice that made Delia shoot a suspicious glance at him. The steward yielded. After giving Craig an identification tag to wear on his shoulder, and pointedly refusing one to Delia, he allowed them both in.

'I could hardly believe that was you talking,' she murmured as they went to their seats.

He grinned. 'I can act the blind man as well as anyone, in a just cause,' he said without irony. 'Get as near the front as you can, and make sure I have an aisle seat.'

'We're coming to steps,' she told him. 'They're shallow and broad, which is awkward because you can't get into a rhythm. *Now*. Then two steps forward, and down.'

He managed the tricky width, his hand tucked in her arm.

'We're here now. Aisle seats.'

'You go in first, so that I'm on the outside.' When they'd seated themselves he said, 'Look around and tell me what you see.'

'It's filling up fast. At this rate it'll be standing room only.'

At last every seat was taken. Lights went up on the stage and seven men trooped on to take their seats behind a long table. Delia described them.

'The one in the middle is fat and jowly, with white hair.'

'That's the chairman, Leabridge. Is there one built

like a string bean with dark hair and a mouth like a trap?'

'Yes, just next to him.'

'The company secretary, Derham. I believe he's behind the labour policy. Leabridge is a buffoon and Derham manipulated him. Now he wants him out so that he can take over, so he's trying to grease his path with money.'

'The chairman's getting up,' Delia said.

'Ready for battle?'

'You bet!'

Delia was fired with excitement. Then she felt a strange sensation in her right hand. For a moment she almost thought Craig had squeezed it, but when she looked his head was turned towards the stage, as though he wasn't aware of her.

CHAPTER SEVEN

AT FIRST very little happened. There was a round of self-congratulatory speeches. Craig sat quietly, waiting for them to finish. Then, when Derham rose, he was on the alert.

Derham's speech was carefully crafted so that the increases he was proposing were almost lost in the verbiage. But Delia, watching Craig, knew that he missed nothing.

At last Derham said, 'Perhaps we could vote on this straight away.'

There was a rumble of agreement from the hall, but Craig broke into it, standing up and facing the platform. 'Before we vote,' he said in a voice pitched to carry, 'there are a few points I think we should consider.'

Derham controlled his irritation at being held up and managed an expression of polite interest. 'I'm sure we would all be interested in hearing your points,' he said.

'You've proposed some very large bonuses for yourselves, and particularly for Mr Leabridge,' Craig said. 'Do you really think the company's recent behaviour justifies this?'

'The company's recent performance has been excellent—' Derham began.

'I didn't say performance,' Craig interrupted him. 'I said *behaviour*.'

'Then I can't imagine what you mean. Profits have never been better—'

'Profits for the board and shareholders perhaps, but the men and women thrown onto the scrap heap haven't got much to celebrate.'

There was a warning in his tone but Derham failed to heed it. 'Regrettably, in the modern industrial age it's been necessary to streamline, to require more work from the employees—'

'But you don't use employees, do you?' Craig said dangerously. 'You use child slaves in countries where you can't be called to account. You're making a fortune on the backs of infants, some as young as six, who live night and day in factories, half starving, and working a fourteen-hour day.'

Leabridge leapt to his feet. 'That is totally false,' he shouted. 'A fabrication got up by a spiteful press.'

A murmur had risen in the hall, but in the face of such a categorical denial it faded. Delia had a moment of apprehension. Surely Craig couldn't have made a mistake.

Then she looked at his face and saw in it an expression of pure delight that reassured her. By denying the charge so completely the chairman had walked right into Craig's trap.

'Mr Chairman,' he said, 'you have told a barefaced lie in front of two thousand people. And I'm going to prove it's a lie. Your own internal documents confirm it.'

He turned so that he faced the audience, and began to reel off facts and figures, refusing to be silenced, charging on like a juggernaut in the face of protests from the platform. He named meetings, listed those present. He seemed to have an uncanny knowledge of who had said what.

Delia didn't have to wait for him to instruct her. She could think ahead, deduce what he needed, and have the relevant file open before his signal. But she was only back-up. He had it all in his head.

A faceless young man who seemed to act as an aide to the chairman jumped to his feet. 'Those are private company matters,' he spluttered. 'They're confidential—'

'Not any more, they aren't,' Craig cried, and the audience roared with laughter. Before it had quite died away he was back in his stride, mowing the opposition down like wrath from heaven.

'As if the present position wasn't bad enough,' he roared, 'there are plans to close yet another factory and move the manufacturing process to a more 'accommodating' country.'

He named the country and detailed some of its abuses. 'The president of that state lives by pocketing backhanders. In return for the right sum he'll provide land, buildings, slave labour, and police who turn a blind eye when children die at the machines. Just how much have you greased his palm so far this year? It wouldn't be a million, would it?'

He was drowned out by shouting, but only for a moment. When he raised his voice it altered, becoming gravelly and powerful. The audience quietened, dominated less by his volume than by the sheer force of his personality.

'Every year that this company has slipped further into the moral mud, its directors have awarded themselves huge bonuses, share options, and anything else their greedy little hearts desire. Now the chairman seeks to smooth his exit with gold. Not so much a golden handshake, more like a golden kick in the rear.'

Leabridge was on his feet again, pale and furious to the point of incoherence. 'You have no right to—nothing is decided—discussions—I will not necessarily be leaving—'

'You will if I have anything to do with it,' Craig informed him, to a round of applause.

After that, the argument moved into a different area and things got extremely technical. Craig needed her help even more now. It took all Delia's concentration to keep up with his demands, calling up files, giving him the necessary information. The men on the platform grew more flustered. They tried to shut Craig up and pass on, but by now the crowd was on his side.

Once, when he'd repeatedly demanded facts against the evasions from the platform, the chairman said, 'I think we've given quite enough time to this matter, and should now pass on to something else.'

'Not so fast!' Craig cried.

'This subject is now closed,' Leabridge intoned, letting his gaze rove around the cinema. 'Any other questions? If not I take it we can—'

'I've got a question.' Delia jumped to her feet.

The chairman regarded her with something like relief. 'Yes, madam? What is it?'

'This,' she said, and proceeded to repeat Craig's last question, word for word. There was laughter and applause, but then someone noticed Delia's lack of a tag.

'Are you a shareholder? If not you shouldn't be on

your feet—most irregular— No, I won't listen to you.'

An elderly lady got to her feet. She looked pink and frail, but her words dispelled that illusion. '*I* am a shareholder,' she said firmly, 'and I want a proper answer to the last question.'

'So do I,' someone called. Another voice was raised, then another, and soon the whole audience was baying for the answer nobody on the platform wanted to give.

A man behind Craig tugged his arm. His identification tag gave his name as Selsdon, and proclaimed him a representative of block shareholders—the ones Craig had said would support the increases for their own greedy motives. It seemed he was right because Selsdon hissed, 'Cut it out for Pete's sake! This will do a lot of damage.'

'Delia?' Craig rapped out.

'Selsdon,' she said, reading. 'Here to represent—' She gave the name of the company.

Craig nodded as though his suspicions had been confirmed. 'Damage to whom?' he demanded of Selsdon.

'All of us. Who wants to rock the boat?'

Craig gave a wolfish, piratical grin. 'I do. And I'm going to keep rocking this particular boat until it capsizes. I advise you to jump ship before your company's name is mud.' His turned his back contemptuously on Selsdon, who sat there, fuming.

The crowd was still calling for an answer. Under cover of the noise Craig demanded some details from the files, and when Delia hesitated he snapped, 'Hurry up! We haven't got all day.'

'Yes, *sir!*'

He seethed with impatience while she tapped at the laptop, finally locating what he wanted. His thanks was a perfunctory grunt, but she felt no resentment. She was thrilled with what he was doing, caught up in the drama, overwhelmed by her admiration for him.

He returned to the fray. The chairman tried to make some sort of reply, got hopelessly bogged down and changed tack.

'This is all very fine and noble,' he sneered at Craig, 'but none of these grand principles have stopped you benefiting as a shareholder, I notice.'

'I bought shares in this company as the only way I could get into shareholder meetings,' Craig snapped. 'I've had one dividend, which I refuse to make use of. It stays in a separate bank account while I try to find a home for it. I've tried to give it to charity, but when I tell them the facts no self-respecting charity will touch it with a barge pole. *Who touches pitch will be defiled.*' His last words were a roar which had the audience cheering.

Delia looked around. Most of the people there were the small shareholders, whose incomes might be affected, yet they were with him, swayed by the force of his honest indignation.

'I propose we vote to deny these monstrous increases,' he cried. 'I further propose a vote of no confidence in this board, and a vote for a total review of its policy.'

The chairman made a dismissive movement, but voices were raised, seconding Craig. At last he had to give in, and the voting started.

'Note down the numbers,' Craig instructed Delia. 'Make certain they're dead accurate.'

Behind them Selsdon was in a rage. 'What the hell am I supposed to do now?' he demanded. 'I've got my instructions from head office. Support the board. But you've made them look immoral. My company's got a good name. It doesn't like being associated with anything dubious.'

'You'll have to follow your conscience,' Craig said ruthlessly. 'Always assuming you and head office can locate it. Hunt about a bit.' Selsdon cast him a look of loathing.

In the end Selsdon faced both ways at once, refusing the vote of no confidence but denying the increases and agreeing to a review of policy. It seemed that a lot of the other company representatives did the same for Craig lost the no-confidence proposal but won the other two. The faces on the platform were pale and strained. The crowd was jubilant. Craig sat back in his seat with a look of grim satisfaction.

Delia turned to him with a glowing face, longing to meet his eyes and exchange the knowledge of their teamwork, and their victory. But there was only blankness there. He was cut off from her admiration and she felt a sudden bitterness, not for herself, but for him. It was so unfair.

Impulsively she seized his hand. 'You did it,' she cried.

He didn't respond in words, but she felt a slight pressure, and this time it was unmistakable. Then he quickly withdrew his hand.

The meeting ended very soon after that. The members of the board couldn't get out fast enough.

'I don't know how I'm going to explain this to head office,' Selsdon muttered.

Somehow Delia got Craig through the mêlée and out to where she'd parked the car. It was hard because everyone wanted to talk to him, slap him on the back, and she guessed that he found it a strain to have these things coming out of the darkness. At last they were safely in the car.

'Home?' she asked.

'Nope.' He gave her an address which she recognised as that of a national paper, and dialled a number on the car phone. 'Jack? We're on our way.' The exhilaration of victory was still in his voice.

'It's a pity you didn't win the no-confidence vote as well,' she sympathised.

'That was inevitable. I only put it in to give the company representatives a minor victory to take back to their head offices. Without that they might have voted down one of the other two, and they were the really important ones.'

'You've got a Machiavellian mind,' she chuckled.

'Thank you,' he said, rightly taking this as a compliment.

Jack turned out to be a battered newshound who'd been on red alert, waiting for Craig's call, seething with frustration at being excluded from the meeting himself. He tapped away eagerly on his computer as Craig tossed out fact after fact, occasionally appealing to Delia for information.

'That's a great story,' Jack said at last. 'Now, a bit about you—'

'No,' Craig said at once. 'This is about the scandal of fat cats living off the suffering of children—'

'And the man who stopped them in their tracks,' Jack protested. 'It's great human interest——'

But Craig was already rising. 'I've given you your story, Jack,' he said firmly. 'If you dare turn me into a circus freak I'll come back here and make you sorry you were born.'

'All right, all right. Look in tomorrow's paper.' He caught his breath. 'That is——'

'Fine. I'll *look*,' Craig said severely. 'Delia, let's go!'

He was quiet on the home journey, but by the time they arrived his mood had improved. Later, he let her cook the supper, and while she was at work he entered the kitchen bearing two glasses of champagne. 'You've earned it,' he said, handing one to her. 'Was I very hard on you?'

'Awful,' she said without rancour. She mimicked him. '"Hurry up! We haven't got all day."'

Craig grinned. 'That's what Alison calls "Daddy being a bear."'

'Not a bear, a lion. You had them all scuttling for cover.'

'I did, didn't I?' he said with grim satisfaction.

'Let's drink to you.' She clinked his glass.

'No, to us. You were wonderful. When you stood up to ask a question I could have wrung your neck for letting them off the hook. Then, when I realised what you were really doing, I could have——well——'

You could have kissed me, she thought. Is that what you were going to say? Her eyes were drawn to his generous, mobile mouth with its firm lips, and she saw them tighten, as though the same idea had occurred to him, only to be rejected. There was a slight flush on his face.

'Anyway, you were marvellous,' he said.

Reluctantly she let it go. Perhaps her moment would come later. It would be useless to try to urge this prickly man to do anything he wasn't sure about. It had always been so easy to make other men do what she wanted, but with Craig it was a whole new territory.

'Supper's almost ready,' she said. 'I'm just about to serve up.'

'Great! I'm famished.' He sounded relieved.

The meal was riotous as they relived their triumph. Afterwards he insisted on helping with the washing up, drying dishes and putting them away accurately.

By the time they returned to the living room he'd mellowed enough to tell her some funny stories about the fights he got involved in, and evidently enjoyed.

'People like we met today don't know how to deal with my blindness, and I make use of that,' he admitted.

'But you hate being perceived as blind.'

'Yes, I do. I won't let Jack use me for 'human interest' fodder, but I'll do what I have to for the sake of those children, even it if means playing up to ignorant preconceptions. What do my problems matter?'

Delia began to laugh.

'What's so funny?'

'That chairman as he scuttled off the platform. And the others chasing him. They all gave you a look of sheer hatred as they went, but they were scared too.'

'That's what I like to hear,' he announced triumphantly.

But even as he said the words the light died from Craig's face, to be replaced by a look of melancholy. He took a deep, shuddering breath. Delia watched him in anguish. By now she was attuned to his mind and could follow what had happened. Tonight he'd made light of his blindness, pretending to use it cynically for his own ends. But it was all a front, and behind it was a wilderness of darkness and despair. His humour was a defence, but the enemy was always waiting to pounce. As it had pounced now.

She couldn't bear it. Tears sprang to her eyes and she reached for him. 'Craig,' she whispered.

He stiffened as she touched his face, and his voice was hard. 'It's all right, Delia. I'm fine.'

'You're not,' she cried passionately. 'Why must you pretend? It's all an act, isn't it? You don't want anyone to know how much you're hurting—'

'But I'm not hurting.' Suddenly he slammed his glass down. 'Damn you, stop this! Who the hell do you think you are?'

'But I only want to help you—'

'You did help me, today, when I wanted it. That kind of help I need, but not what you're offering now. Tears and pity—' A tremor went through him. 'I'm going to bed.'

He rose quickly and strode out into the hall. But his anger had confused him. He missed his footing on the bottom step, stumbled, clutched the bannister and fell on the steps. Delia flew to help him.

Don't touch me!' he shouted.

She stayed where she was, a foot away from him, scared to move or even speak while Craig was mentally thrashing around in his private nightmare.

'If you know what's good for you, don't come near me,' he said at last in a shaking voice. 'Do you hear? *Where are you?*'

'I'm here,' she said quickly. 'I'm not coming any closer. I'm going right away from you. I promise.'

She took a few steps back, and watched unhappily as he picked himself up, located the bannister with his hand and began to climb the stairs. She couldn't move until the door of his room had closed behind him. Then she stumbled back to the sofa and collapsed on it, her head in her hands, rocking back and forth in anguish.

She knew the truth about herself at that moment, and it was dreadful. Beneath a pretty face she was nothing, just a vacuum. Because when the man who increasingly touched her heart needed help she was useless to him. There was nothing in her that could make him reach out to her in his pain, and take comfort from her presence. There was nothing of value in her at all. She'd suspected it for a long time, but she knew it now.

She lay awake half the night, trying not to shiver at the thoughts that had risen up to taunt her. But Craig had forced her to face the terrible truth that she'd avoided for years. She wondered how she could endure staying in this house, where there was nowhere to hide from herself.

All at once she sat up, wondering if she was imagining things, or if she really could hear shouting from along the corridor. The next moment there was a crash. Delia leapt out of bed and rushed to Craig's room. When she snapped the light on she could see

that his bedside radio lay on the floor. Craig himself
was standing in the middle of the room, reaching out
around him in a frantic effort to find some firm object.
He wore only pyjama trousers, and his bare chest
heaved with his distress.

'Craig!' she cried.

He turned to her. His face was livid. 'Where am I?'
he demanded. *'Where the hell am I?'*

'Keep still.' She took his hand and he seized her
convulsively.

'I had a bad dream,' he gasped. 'I must have got
up while I was still asleep—I've lost my bearings—'

'It's all right. Put your hand on my shoulder.'

She guided his hand around her shoulders and put
her free arm about his waist. He was trembling violently and without thinking what she was doing she
instinctively slipped her other arm about him as well
holding him firmly in a gesture of consolation. His
grip tightened and he clung onto her like a drowning
man with a straw. Delia felt herself pressed against
him, absorbing the heat from his body, and she was
suddenly very aware of how little she was wearing.
Her low-cut nightdress was made of the sheerest silk,
so that there was almost nothing between her nakedness and his.

He sensed it in the same moment. She felt his sudden tension as his hands brushed against her skin with
its gossamer covering. Before, he'd only touched her
face. Now he was finding her slim shape, its elegant
curves, its seductiveness.

Time seemed to stop. Delia was intensely aware of
every part of him at the same moment. She'd admired
his body in the gym, but only at a distance. Being

held close to it was an experience that left her trembling. She could feel the hard, lean length of him pressed against her, and with it was the unmistakable intimation that he'd discovered her as a woman.

Delia's head swam with the intensity of the feelings that coursed through her. If he'd found her as a woman, she'd found him as a man, and with a completeness that was almost shocking. They'd been careful, treating each other with caution. Yet this had been waiting all the time, ready to come alive when their guards were down. Now it was too late. She wanted him. She wanted everything. She wanted his lips on her mouth, his arms about her body. She wanted him in her bed, caressing her, claiming her.

Craig began moving his hands tentatively, letting his fingers trace a soft line down her cheek, her long neck, over the curves and valleys of her shape, causing tremors of unbearable excitement to go through her. Until now her body had existed for others to gaze at and appreciate, but now suddenly it existed for herself. It had been created so that this one man could bring it to joyful life.

He was only stroking her gently, but his lightest touch affected her more than another man's kiss would have done. Half-unconsciously she pressed against him, lifting her face so that her warm breath caressed his skin. She moved her fingers lightly on his naked back, not drawing him closer but sending him soft messages of intimacy. In another moment he would surely tighten his arms and kiss her.

But then she saw Craig's face. It was desperate. Something that to her was a joyful revelation was, to him, a terrible weakness. He wanted her, but he didn't *want* to want her. He would fight his desire like an enemy.

At last a shudder went through him and his hands dropped. The battle was over and he'd won, at a terrible cost to them both. He wanted to pretend it hadn't happened, and if she seemed aware of his 'weakness' he would never forgive her.

'Come with me,' she forced herself to say. 'Your bed is over here.'

Slowly she guided him, letting him feel the edge of the bed against his legs. He snatched his hands away from her and sat, feeling around for the cabinet, the bedhead, anything that was familiar.

Delia picked up the radio and tried not to let her voice shake with the strength of her emotion. 'You must have lashed out in your dream, and knocked the radio onto the floor. I heard the crash.'

'Did you—hear anything else?'

'Yes, I heard you shout. That must have been the dream.'

'I owe you an apology,' he said politely. 'I was very rude to you tonight.'

Her heart sank at his formal tone. She longed to assure him she didn't mind his rough behaviour, but he would interpret that as being patronising.

'You were pretty rotten,' she agreed. 'But it doesn't worry me any more.'

He gave an awkward grin. 'How about making me a cup of tea? I don't think I could manage it myself right now.'

When she returned with a tray of tea and two cups, she'd covered herself with a dressing gown. Craig had put on a pyjama jacket and dressing gown, and was sitting in a chair. She poured his cup and set it by his elbow. He thanked her, said something by way of small talk and she answered in the same vein. She knew that he was re-establishing their relationship on a prosaic footing, with the distance between them increased by the moment of blazing awareness that had caught them both.

Delia looked around her, taking in the details of his room. It was spartan, almost bleak. The unusually large bed was made of pine, as was the wardrobe and dressing table. Against the far wall she saw something that made her catch her breath sharply.

'What is it?' Craig demanded at once.

'Nothing, I—it's just—the dog basket—it's so sad and empty.'

'Yes,' he said heavily. 'Not that Jenny spends much time in it. Mostly she sleeps on the bed. Guide dogs are trained not to, but Jenny and I decided to ignore that bit. We like being together. That's why the bed's so wide. She just takes the space she wants and leaves me to make do with the rest. I got tired of clinging onto the edge so I bought one big enough for three.'

The next moment a glance of sadness crossed his face, as though he was thinking of the lonely nights without the warm, comforting presence.

'But you'll have her back soon, won't you?' she asked urgently.

It seemed a long time before he said, 'I don't know. If she can't overcome her fear of traffic I'll have to have another dog. But I don't want another. I want *her*.' His voice shook.

'Another dog wouldn't be the same,' he went on after a moment. 'Jenny and I have years of trust and love that we've built up. We knew from the very first moment that we were right for each other.' He gave a forced laugh. 'I guess that sounds pretty sentimental.'

'No. Why shouldn't you love her when she's so good to you? But surely she'll get her nerve back, with rest and retraining?'

'She's eight years old. That's elderly for a dog. It may simply be too much of a struggle for her. I'm going to visit her at the training centre this weekend. Maybe that will help. I don't know.'

'That's fine,' Delia said eagerly. 'I'm looking forward to meeting her properly.'

After an awkward silence Craig said, 'My usual driver is going to take me. There's no need to trouble you.'

Delia drew in a slow breath, wondering if she would ever get used to the pain of being snubbed. 'You mean you don't want me around Jenny, don't you?' she asked in a mortified voice.

'Delia, don't take it personally—'

'How else can I take it? Don't you realise that the last time I saw Jenny she was lying unconscious in the vet's surgery? I can't get that picture out of my mind. But perhaps I'd be able to if I saw her looking well. I might begin to feel less of a monster. But as far as you're concerned I'm still beyond the pale, aren't I?'

'Don't be silly,' he said roughly. 'I don't mean that at all. I may have had a few uncharitable thoughts about you at first, but we're past that now. I didn't think you'd want to come—'

'Of course I do. I want— Oh, *hell*!' She set down

her cup sharply and rested her forehead in her hands.
The words she wanted to say wouldn't come. He
would probably think them stupid.

After a moment she felt the light touch of his fingers on her hair. 'Delia? Are you all right?'

'Yes, I'm all right,' she said gruffly. She wanted to
take hold of one of his hands, turn her head and rub
her cheek against it. But she resisted the temptation.

'Does this really mean so much to you?'

'More than you'll ever know. You see, I want—I
want to ask Jenny to forgive me,' she whispered.

'All right,' he said after a moment. 'In that case—
I'll be glad if you'll come with me.'

CHAPTER EIGHT

JACK had done them proud. The story that appeared in next morning's paper was calculated to make the chairman and board shake in their shoes. Delia read it to Craig over breakfast.

'Are you sure he hasn't put in anything sickening about me?' Craig demanded suspiciously.

'He hasn't even mentioned that you're blind,' Delia reassured him.

'Good. Then I hope I've started a riot. With any luck their shares will be plunging in an hour.' He grinned. 'I feel ready for a good day.'

'So do I.' She drank her coffee and looked out of the window. 'Your driver's here. I must dash.'

She reached the office to find Helen urgently awaiting her arrival. 'Brian called a meeting yesterday afternoon,' she said. 'He came in here looking for you.'

'I told him I was taking a day's leave. I suppose Mark was at this meeting?'

'And Mr Gorham. Brian told him he simply couldn't imagine where you were.'

'Then I think I'll have a word with Brian,' Delia seethed, and headed along the corridor.

But Brian was all prepared. 'Delia, I'm so sorry. Of course you did tell me you were going to be absent, and I—somewhat reluctantly—agreed.'

'You never said anything about being reluctant,' she protested.

'I think I did. I *think* I mentioned that there was a lot of work on at the moment, and it wasn't really convenient. But it's no matter. You're here now, and I'm sure you'll soon catch up. Mark will fill you in about our meeting yesterday.'

Delia bit back the hot words that sprang to her lips. It could do no good now. For the next hour she had to endure the mortification of being briefed by Mark at his most insufferable.

The one pleasure the day held was that of watching the news on her office television. The story was growing by the minute and the shares were diving, as Craig had predicted. Leabridge, panic-stricken, was backtracking and announcing policy reviews every five minutes.

Brian looked into her office at the end of the day. 'I'd like you to read through these papers,' he said, placing them on her desk. 'They're rather important, so you won't mind if I call you about them tomorrow, during the day.'

'But tomorrow is Saturday. I'm sorry, Brian, but I'm busy all day.'

'Indeed. Indeed. I should have thought that in view of— However, as you say, it's Saturday, and of course your personal life is your own.'

'I beg your pardon?'

'A beautiful young woman doesn't want to spend all her life working. I'm sure there's a boyfriend in the picture somewhere. Love has its claims.'

'I'll read the papers on Sunday and see you first thing Monday morning,' Delia said stiffly.

'I'm afraid you'll be seeing me sooner than that. Tomorrow evening is the P.R. Associates dinner.

Remember?' Brian said, whisking them away. 'Don't let the papers trouble you. Mark and I can manage.'

Delia watched him go, realising that she'd handed him and Mark a victory. But she had no choice. Tomorrow she was taking Craig to visit Jenny, and nothing was more important than that.

Craig told her more about Jenny as they drove to the centre.

'She was given to me by The Guide Dogs for the Blind Association. They train a young dog for about eight months until it knows all the things it has to do, like stopping, starting, waiting at kerbs, judging distances. But the hard part is matching a dog with the right owner.

'I went to stay for a month in the place we're going to now. When I'd settled into my room I heard the door open and close again. The next moment there was fur brushing against my hand, and a cold nose pressing against my cheek. I felt her all over, and her tail was wagging like mad. She was beautiful. I knew at once that we were perfect together, and so did she.

'When we started working as a team everything went right. That doesn't always happen. Some teams have to work a long time before they get it right. But we were completely in tune at once. Since then she's been part of my life; not just my eyes, but my friend. I can tell her things I wouldn't tell anyone else.' He said this simply, genuinely.

At last they turned into a quiet road. The training centre was a collection of low buildings. Craig directed her to the right one from memory. When they were inside he said, 'We have to find Hilda Mullins' office. Let's see if I can remember the way.'

He managed it at first, but then became lost. 'Curse it!' he said fretfully. 'I was so sure I could— What was that?' A bark had reached them from around the corner. 'That's Jenny,' he said excitedly.

'Craig,' she protested, laughing. 'There must be so many dogs here.'

'No, it's *her*. I'd know her bark if there were a million others. Hilda said she'd have her in her office, ready for me. Follow that bark.'

It was coming more insistently now, infused with a note of agitated delight.

'Perhaps she heard your voice,' Delia said, making her way around the corner. The excitement was getting to her too.

At last she found the door and knocked. A pleasant voice from inside said, 'Come in.'

Hilda was a middle-aged woman with a warm smile. She rose at once, but her greeting was lost in the commotion made by a yellow Labrador, who scurried forward, her tail going nineteen to the dozen, and was enfolded in Craig's arms. Her delight was reflected on his face as he patted her, scratched her head and murmured in her ear.

When at last the two had finished greeting each other Craig straightened up and said to Delia, 'This is Jenny.'

She took a deep breath and leaned down. To her relief Jenny didn't back away from her, but looked up with soft brown eyes. On the night of the accident Delia had noticed in passing that this was a lovely dog, but now she could see just how lovely. She was a pale honey colour, with a broad head, thick silky fur and an expression of benevolence. Delia had last seen her lying unconscious on the surgery table. Now Jenny was bright, friendly and apparently confident. It seemed impossible that anything could still be wrong with her, and Delia dropped to her knees and embraced her with relief.

'I'm sorry,' she whispered. 'I'm so sorry.'

Jenny placed her chin confidingly in Delia's hand, looking slightly puzzled, as if wondering what there was to be sorry about. Of course, she'd seen only the car, not the driver, Delia thought. But still she was passionately thankful at what felt like a gesture of forgiveness.

Over tea Hilda explained Jenny's problems.

'Most of the time she seems fine. She can do everything as she used to, including walking in the street, sometimes. But then suddenly she'll get a panic attack at the kerb.'

'I'm afraid that's my fault,' Delia confessed. 'I was driving the car that struck her.' She forced herself to continue. 'I mounted the pavement. She didn't have a chance.'

Hilda hesitated briefly, but her voice was still friendly as she asked, 'Do you have the same car today?'

'Yes.'

'Then we can see how she reacts to it. But first I think Mr Locksley should work with her, so that they can get used to each other again.'

When Craig bent down to fix her harness on Jenny gave a beaming grin, as if saying that this was how things were supposed to be. They all went outside, and Delia watched with Miss Mullins as the two of them went through their paces. Jenny performed everything asked of her with quiet authority.

'Now let's see her take you between us,' Hilda said to Craig. 'Delia, will you stand just inside this doorway, and I'll do the same on the other side, so there's just a narrow gap between us? Craig, the doorway is just in front of you. See if she'll take you through.'

'Forward,' Craig commanded.

Jenny considered, then sat down.

'Forward,' Craig repeated.

Jenny didn't budge.

'Well done!' Hilda cried.

'It's good that she disobeyed?' Delia asked.

'With you crowding that doorway, the gap must be too small for me,' Craig explained. 'Jenny knows exactly how wide my shoulders are, and if there's no room she won't move. Well done, girl. You remembered that perfectly.'

The grounds were set up with tests for going round obstacles, and even a simulated street, with helpers driving vehicles. Jenny sailed through everything.

'Shall we try it with my car?' Delia said.

Craig went to stand with Jenny on the edge of the kerb. Delia got behind her wheel and began to drive forward slowly. As she drew close she saw Craig's lips move in the command, 'Forward.' Jenny studied the road, then stayed motionless. There was no doubt that she'd seen the car, but beyond becoming rooted to the spot she didn't react. Craig reached down and touched her, and Delia just had time to notice his smile as she went past.

'How was it?' she asked eagerly when she'd run back.

'Fine. She didn't shake or show any signs of distress,' Craig said jubilantly. 'We're getting there, Jenny. You'll soon be home.'

He knelt down to pet the dog, who received his caresses ecstatically. Delia watched them with delight.

Hilda was more restrained. 'It's fine,' she said, 'but that was the easy bit. It'll be much harder on the roads.'

'I know.' Craig straightened up. 'I'll take her out now, while she's doing so well.'

'Perhaps I'd better come with you, just in case,' Hilda suggested.

'I'll go,' Delia said at once.

'You can leave me in Delia's safe hands,' Craig said wryly. 'If there are any problems, she'll bring me back. But there won't be any. Jenny's her old self, aren't you, girl?'

Jenny gave a bark of agreement, and the three of them set off cheerfully for the gate. Delia kept her distance from the other two, thrilled at how perfectly they were working again. A weight was lifting from her conscience.

They left the entrance behind, heading for the main road. As they turned into it Craig called, 'There's a big set of traffic lights just here. I'm going to tell her to cross.'

Delia didn't answer. She was watching Jenny, troubled by a change that had come over the dog. She was walking normally, but suddenly her tail had drooped.

At the edge of the pavement they halted. Craig

pressed the button that worked the lights, and listened for the sound that would tell him it was safe to cross. At last it came.

'Come on, Jenny,' he said. 'Let's show 'em. Forward.' But Jenny didn't move. 'Forward,' Craig said again, louder.

When there was no response he spoke to Delia. 'Is there something coming? Is that why she's refusing?'

'All the traffic has stopped at the lights,' Delia said.

He bent to touch the dog, and immediately felt what was wrong. Jenny was shivering so violently that Delia could see it from a few feet away. Craig was very pale.

'All right,' he said quietly. 'Back.' He gave a slight tug on the harness and Jenny stepped back from the edge of the pavement. 'I guess we'd better give this up,' he said heavily.

Jenny gave a soft whimper, and at once his hand was on her head, caressing her gently. 'All right, girl. Not your fault.'

They returned in silence. Hilda received them sympathetically. She said little while Craig consoled Jenny. The dog responded, rubbing her head against his hand, but she looked drained and miserable. She'd failed at the work to which her whole life had been dedicated. Above all she'd failed her beloved master, and her sadness and confusion were there in her eyes.

'It's too soon to give up hope,' Hilda said gently. 'We'll keep her here for a while, and hope it comes back to her.'

There was a silence. In the end it was Delia who asked, 'And if it doesn't?'

'It will,' Craig said at once.

'I'm sure it will,' Hilda said. 'But if not I'm afraid you'll have to have another dog.'

'And give up Jenny?' Craig asked in a strained voice.

'What would happen to her?' Delia asked. 'She wouldn't be put down?'

'Certainly not,' Hilda said firmly. 'We never put down healthy dogs, just retire them to new homes.'

'I won't let her go to strangers,' Craig said at once. 'She'd hate it. She knows she belongs with me.'

Hilda thought for a moment. 'You don't live alone, do you? My notes say you've got a daughter, and someone who comes in every day.'

'That's right.'

'And quite a large house and garden. You could cope with two dogs.'

'You mean I could keep her as a pet?' Craig asked eagerly.

'Possibly. It's not ideal, but it sometimes works.'

A sick feeling was overtaking Delia as she listened. 'But what would Jenny do during the day?' she asked. 'She's used to coming to work with you, and being with you all the time. She'd have to be left behind—like a reject.'

Craig turned his head in her direction, a quizzical look on his face. 'That's a bit melodramatic, isn't it?' he said.

'Perhaps. I just think she'd feel it when you left the house with another dog wearing *her* harness.'

'We'll do everything we can to get her confidence back,' Hilda said. 'But she's not young. This may be the best compromise. Don't worry about it for the moment.'

It was time to go. Craig held out a hand to Jenny who came to him eagerly.

'Goodbye, old girl,' he murmured. 'I'll come again soon. Be good.'

He gave her a final pat, and went to the door. Jenny looked after him, a bewildered expression on her face. A soft whimper broke from her throat as she realised Craig was leaving her behind. True to her training, she didn't try to follow, or protest. She merely sat there forlornly as her master went away.

Craig didn't seem to want to talk as they drove home, and Delia was glad. She was full of misery—a feeling that started with Jenny's fate but went beyond it.

She made them both a light meal when they got in, but then sat staring at her plate.

'What is it?' Craig asked at last. 'You've been quiet ever since we left the centre. Is it Jenny? She's going to be fine.'

'No, she isn't,' Delia said fiercely. 'Not if she's relegated to second-best because she couldn't measure up. It'll break her heart. You can't let her—you don't understand.' Her voice was becoming thick with tears as she struggled to find the words. 'You didn't see her face as you left, but I did and—oh, God, what have I done?' She broke down and wept unrestrainedly.

Craig was thunderstruck. He'd heard her weep once before, on the first night, but that had been a reaction from overstretched nerves. Her grief for the suffering of another creature was something different.

After a moment he stroked her hair with gentle fingers. 'Don't cry, Delia. It'll come right.'

'Suppose it doesn't?' she asked huskily. 'How will she bear it?'

'But Jenny's a dog. You don't know what she's feeling.'

'I do. I saw it in her eyes, and—I know. It happened to me, and I *know*.'

'What do you mean, it happened to you?'

'I—I can't explain.'

'Yes, you can. Tell me.'

When she didn't answer he took a firm hold of her and drew her to her feet, propelling her into the living room and towards the sofa. 'Now, you're going to tell me what's upsetting you,' he insisted. 'And we'll see what can be done about it.'

'All right, I'll tell you. I know you despise me as a vain, shallow woman who thinks of nothing but her looks and the admiration she can get.'

'I don't despise you—'

'It's been more like a curse to me, right from the start. From the moment I was old enough to understand words I heard about nothing but my looks. My father was so proud of me—no, of *them*. I've got a sister, a year younger. She's bright and clever, and nice-looking, but he didn't give her half as much attention as me, because I was *the family beauty*.' Delia said the last words in a scathing tone that made Craig turn his head sharply to catch every nuance of her voice.

'Go on,' he said.

'It was fine at first, being Daddy's darling, able to wrap him round my little finger. But he became obsessive. I was a child model because that was what he wanted.'

'What about your mother?'

'She wasn't happy but my father just steamrollered over her. He was the one who came to photographic shoots with me. He loved basking in all the attention. I ended up with a crowded schedule and no time to be young.'

'That's why you got so annoyed for Alison?'

'Yes. There were so many childish pleasures I missed out on because he'd booked me in somewhere. He took on far too many engagements and I got exhausted. One day, when I couldn't take any more, I threw a screaming tantrum right in the middle of a shoot. Nobody would hire me again, and he was furious with me.'

Her voice became husky. 'After that I wasn't his pride and joy any more. He just lost interest in me. He discovered that my sister could act. He had contacts by then, and he used them to push her into commercials, so after that she had all his attention. I used to watch them go off together—do you see...?'

'Yes,' he said softly. 'I see.'

'I'd thought he really loved me, that I was special to him. But I wasn't—not really...'

Craig listened to the silence. When it wasn't broken he reached for her. His hands touched her shoulder and he tensed when he felt it shaking.

'Are you still crying?' he asked in wonder.

'No—no—it's just—I've started remembering things I've tried not to think of for years.'

'Your father really stopped loving you for a reason like that?'

'It wasn't *me* he loved. It was my face, and the exciting life it could give him. For a while I hated my own looks. I played them down, tried to hide them. But then I started to grow up, and realised that looks could have their advantages, so I began making the best of myself, only this time I did it for me.

'Oh, there are a thousand ways. There are smiles, and turns of the head, and glances through your lashes. And men get dizzy looking at you and forget they were going to give you a parking ticket, or they let you jump the queue. It's easy and it's cheap, and soon your whole life is like that, and there's nothing else...'

'Why are you so hard on yourself?' he asked gently. 'Is it because I was hard on you?'

'You had every right to be,' she cried. 'Everything you said about me is true.'

'Nothing I said about you that night is true. I spoke in anger, and I didn't know you then.'

'You knew me better than anyone,' she said with self-condemning bitterness. 'You were the one person I couldn't fool.'

'Delia, don't talk like this. Don't make yourself out to be a monster just because you got a little confused.'

Craig had reached out his hand. Delia clung to it as though it were her salvation, trying to sort out her thoughts. She'd told him part of the story, but there were no words to express the bewildered anguish of discovering that the father she'd adored had loved her for the most superficial reasons—which meant he hadn't really loved her at all. His later indifference had filled her with fear in case other men should also learn her terrible secret—*that she was worthless inside.*

She'd polished up the glossy surface so that nobody

could see beneath it. But then she'd met Craig, to whom the surface meant nothing. He'd judged her harshly, reviving the demons that haunted her. If only she could find the way to explain it all to him. But perhaps the man whose blind eyes saw so much would know without words.

'I'm glad you told me all this,' he said at last. 'Now I know why your face was so tense and haunted when we first met. But that seems a long time ago.'

'And—now?' she asked breathlessly.

'Now it's different: gentle and kind, the way nature meant it to be.'

'But how can you know? You've never touched my face since that night, when you told me all the things that you disliked about it.'

'I didn't dislike it. I was just troubled that it was being spoiled by something wrong inside you. But since then I've heard echoes in your voice—kindness and compassion, and—other things. I know you're good and lovely inside because you turned your own pain into care for my daughter. I know your features are softer, and your eyes glow. If I touched your face now I'd find it truly beautiful, as I understand beauty.'

'Why don't you?' she whispered.

He gave a sigh that was half a shudder. 'Because it would make me want you too much.'

'Would that be so bad?'

'Yes. You know—you are not for me.'

She whispered, 'I am, if you want me.'

He was silent and still racked by indecision. Delia drew his fingers up and laid them against her cheek. A tremor went through him. He would have pulled away from her, but he was helpless. Slowly he began to touch her face.

Her eyes were large, fringed with heavy, silky lashes. Her eyebrows too were heavy. He could guess how they dominated her face, giving it dramatic impact. With one finger he traced her straight, delicate nose with its precisely perfect length.

Her mouth was a revelation, wide and generously curved. He'd imagined it like that, thought of how it would feel to kiss it, and now the temptation to do so was tormenting him.

Delia hardly dared to move but her heart was beating wildly. Ever since the night she'd heard him calling and had gone to him, she'd longed for Craig to touch her.

At the back of her mind had been the half-conscious hope that his perception of her beauty would bring him too under her spell, and she would feel safe again, in a world where she understood the rules.

But as his fingers drifted softly across her features she knew that she was deluding herself. His touch did something magical to her, something no other man's touch had ever done, and she wanted it to go on happening. Inside her everything was dissolving into warmth and happiness. If only she could stay like this with him for ever.

The feel of his fingers, tracing the outline of her lips, was devastating. Tremors went through her. Only half knowing what she did, she placed her hands at either side of his face, holding them there for a moment before drawing his head closer to hers.

Craig groaned as he felt the last of his control drain

away. All his wiser instincts warned him he was doing something he would regret, but nothing in the world could have stopped him. He'd fought his desire too long, and he couldn't fight it any longer.

Her lips burned him. They were soft and yielding, warm with promise, suggesting everything, making him want everything. All caution was forgotten. He was filled now with awareness of her, only of her. He moved his mouth over hers, tasting her sweetness.

'Delia...' His murmur of her name was almost inaudible, yet she heard it and thrilled to the wondering note she sensed there. She couldn't answer because his kiss had deepened, become hungry, as though all his pent-up desire and emotion had broken out at last.

Their constraint was falling away, leaving only a man and a woman, in each other's arms because they were in each other's hearts; and Delia rejoiced as she felt herself coming home at last.

But the next moment she felt him stiffen in resistance. Then she felt his hands, firm on her shoulders, pushing her away reluctantly, but insistently.

'Craig...' she protested softly.

'You shouldn't have done that, Delia. It's not kind to torment me.'

'Do you really think that's what I was doing? Playing with you, just to prove that I have some sort of power? Craig, you can't believe me capable of that. You *can't*.'

He gave a groan. 'No—not that. But you don't know what it's like in the dark. You don't understand how everything lovely becomes a torment because it's always taken away.'

'But I'm not going away,' she said, putting her

arms about his neck and laying her lips on his again.
'I want this, Craig,' she murmured. 'I want *you*.'

Now he didn't resist, but drew her back into the
circle of his arms. She came eagerly, offering up
everything she had or was to this man whose hold on
her heart was so painful, yet so strong. It was like
being kissed for the first time, a revelation of what a
kiss could be, and this time nothing was going to prevent her claiming her love.

CHAPTER NINE

THE shrill of the doorbell shattered their dream. It was a cruel interruption, and for a moment they clung together, trying to believe it wasn't happening. But the loud ringing came again, unrelenting, offering no escape.

'Whoever's there isn't going to go away,' Delia sighed. 'Let's hope it's someone I can put off.'

But the man who stood outside was Laurence, wearing evening rig and an irritated expression.

'Whatever are you doing here?' Delia gasped.

'What are *you* doing here? Why aren't you at home, waiting for me to collect you, as we arranged?'

'Oh, heavens!' Delia's hand flew to her mouth as memory returned. 'That!'

'Yes, that.' Laurence brushed past her into the house. 'Only one of the most important evenings in your calendar. And you forgot all about it, didn't you?'

She had indeed forgotten about the annual dinner given by the Public Relations Associates. It was held at a top West End hotel, and was a gathering of all the most notable names in the business. Delia always made a point of attending, knowing that she would make vital contacts. But tonight it had gone right out of her head.

'Who is it?' Craig called.

Reluctantly Delia allowed Laurence to pass her. He

marched confidently into the house and headed straight for the room where Craig had risen from the sofa. He was pale but composed. Delia introduced the two men. Craig held out his hand, but instead of simply shaking it naturally Laurence set down the large suitcase he was carrying and encased Craig's hand in both of his, shaking it earnestly.

'I'm really delighted to meet you,' he said in a slow, hushed voice that suggested he was talking to a mental incompetent, and which Delia knew would infuriate Craig. 'Delia's told me so much about you.'

He released Craig's hand and said, 'Won't you sit down?' as though this were his own house instead of Craig's.

Craig ignored the suggestion. 'What's happened, Delia?'

'Nothing for you to worry about,' Laurence broke in before she could speak. 'A small contretemps that Delia and I can easily put right. There's no need for you to be concerned.'

'Delia?' Craig asked sharply.

'I forgot I was supposed to be going to some function tonight. I'm sorry, Laurence, but it went right out of my head. Will you mind very much going without me?'

'There's no need for that,' Laurence assured her with irritating smoothness. 'We've just got time if you hurry.'

'I haven't got a suitable dress here.'

'So I anticipated. That's why I collected one from your flat.' He opened the suitcase and pulled out a slinky red creation with a great deal of glitter.

Delia was too distracted to notice Craig's slight

stiffening at the news that Laurence was in a position to enter her flat and go through her clothes. 'I'm sorry I forgot, really I am,' she said. 'But I simply can't come now.'

'Nonsense. You must. Think of the useful people you'll meet.'

'Naturally you'll go, Delia,' Craig said quietly. 'I won't hear of you missing it. I'm only sorry I was the cause of you forgetting.'

She looked at him in despair. How could he send her away at a moment like this, when together they'd come so close to the gate of heaven? Did it mean nothing to him?

'Hurry up and get changed,' Laurence urged, holding out the dress.

'Not into that,' Delia said, regarding it with horror. How could she ever have worn such a deliberately provocative creation, so skin-tight, so low-cut over the bosom, so high-slit up the side? She'd bought it at a time when she'd regarded her looks as no more than a useful asset, and now the man who'd taught her better was standing there, every line of his body tense. Luckily he couldn't see the vulgar garment, but how much could he guess?

'What's wrong with it?' Laurence demanded peevishly.

'It's not—suitable,' she hedged. She threw him a frantic glance to make him stop this, but either Laurence didn't see it or he didn't understand it.

'Why isn't it suitable?' he persisted.

'It's so tight and—and low in the front. I need something more demure.' Delia lowered her voice, but Craig's sharp ears still caught every word.

Laurence gave a crack of laughter. 'Demure? For that lot? They don't know what demure is. This dress is perfect: a bit low-cut perhaps, but you can afford that. If you've got it, flaunt it, I say. You've never minded flaunting it before.'

Delia felt herself going hot with shame. It was like seeing her previous self paraded before her. 'I want to get something else,' she said, trying to sound firm.

'Darling, you haven't got the time,' Laurence said with the kind of patience that was really impatience. 'We'll only just make it if we leave now.'

'Go and change, Delia,' Craig said quietly. 'I'm sure the dress will look charming on you.'

'Craig,' she appealed to him, 'you don't know what it's like.'

'I can imagine,' he said quietly.

Snatching the garment from Laurence, she ran up the stairs.

'Can I get you a drink?' Craig asked calmly.

'Thanks. Just a ginger ale, if you have it. Got to be careful when I'm driving Delia. Precious cargo. Know what I mean?'

'Exactly,' Craig said in a voice that gave nothing away.

'Perhaps I'd better pour it.'

'Thank you, I know my way around my own drinks cabinet.' Craig touched the bottles until he found the right one, and filled a glass.

'Hey, you got it just right,' Laurence said admiringly. 'Wish I knew how you do that. Dead clever.'

Out of sight Craig clenched his hands until the knuckles were white, but his voice was cool and emo-

tionless. 'You're too kind,' he said. 'I've trained myself to do a good deal. I can even eat without help.'

Laurence stared, then light dawned and he gave a
guffaw. 'That was a joke, right? Very good. Very
good. Well, so this is where Delia's been shutting
herself away from the world. Not a bad little place, I
must say. Not bad at all. Of course, my Delia's got
an overgrown conscience. Oh, yes. She was very cut
up about what happened. Anything she could do to
put it right, and all that. Mind you, I doubt if she
realised then—well, anyway...'

Craig's voice was hard. 'If you're suggesting that
I pressured her you've made a big mistake.'

'No, no, I never meant that,' Laurence said in a
voice that was supposed to be soothing, but which
grated on his listener like metal on glass. 'But she's
a bit impetuous. Take tonight, for instance. The annual dinner of PR Associates. A big night for her, and
what happens? She forgets it, and that's not like Delia.
Getting on in the world is the only thing that matters
to her.'

'You do her an injustice. These things are only on
the surface. Underneath is the real Delia, a gentle,
beautiful woman.'

Laurence laughed. 'Well, we all know she's beautiful. Hey, how did *you* know?'

'It doesn't matter,' Craig said quietly. 'I know.'

At last they heard her footsteps, making a slight
click that told Craig she'd changed into high heels.
Of course she would, he thought. Only high heels
would go with that tight-fitting, low-cut dress that he
was picturing so painfully.

'I won't be long,' she said to Craig.

'Nonsense,' he said quickly. 'You must stay late and make as many contacts as you can. I won't hear of you throwing your chances away.'

'They'll all want to meet my girl,' Laurence declared. Delia wished he'd stop calling her his, in front of Craig. Then something even worse happened.

'Before we leave, you must put this on,' Laurence declared, opening a flat box. 'I bought it to go with that dress. It's a ruby necklace,' he added kindly, for Craig's benefit.

'I can't take it; it's much too expensive,' Delia protested.

'You're worth all the money in the world,' he stated. 'Naturally I bought the best for you.' He was fixing it around her neck as he spoke. 'It looks great,' he announced. 'Nice and heavy, and V-shaped. It follows the line of your cleavage, and it'll knock their eyes out.'

Delia felt as if she was moving through a nightmare. She managed a mechanical smile, and Laurence, taking this as encouragement, gave her a noisy kiss.

'Mmm, who'll have the biggest beauty on his arm tonight?' he murmured against her neck.

'Laurence, *please...*' she whispered vehemently.

'No need to be shy, darling.'

'If you're late you should leave quickly,' Craig broke in. It was impossible to tell from his voice what he was feeling. 'Goodnight, Delia.'

'Alison hasn't called yet,' she said in final protest.

'When she does I'll explain to her. I'm sure she won't begrudge you an evening's enjoyment.' He turned and walked away, leaving Delia looking after him in helpless anguish.

When Laurence had eased his gleaming car into the traffic a few minutes later he said, 'I can't believe you actually forgot, especially considering what might hang on it.'

'Hang on it?'

'Don't tell me you've forgotten that too. The award, for Pete's sake! You had enough to say about it when you were putting in your entry.'

'No, I hadn't forgotten,' she said quickly. It would have been useless to try to make him understand how far away it all seemed. The Associates had its own awards scheme, and Delia had entered the New Product category with a promotion she'd done on a new Orchid line the previous year. Mark had entered the same category with some work he'd done in his previous employment. So they were in direct competition. Once that would have seemed terribly important.

'I don't think your flatmate likes me,' Laurence was saying. 'She let me in, but very reluctantly.'

'I'm surprised Maggie let you go through my wardrobe.'

'She didn't. I described the dress I wanted and she fetched it. I made the right choice, too. You look stunning, Delia. Delia?'

'Sorry. I was miles away.'

'I said you look stunning. Exactly like I expect my girl to look.'

'Thank you, Laurence. I'm glad you feel I do you credit.'

* * *

The hotel ballroom had been designed to suggest a palace, with gilt and cream decor, heavy brocade curtains and glittering chandeliers. Laurence and Delia were among the last to arrive. Nearly a thousand people were there, dressed to the nines, drinking, talking, laughing too loud at each other's familiar jokes.

'We've just got time for one drink before dinner,' Laurence declared.

'I'll have a mineral water,' Delia said.

'That's not what you usually—'

'Just a mineral water, please.'

'Suit yourself. I hope you're not going to spoil this evening by sulking. You ought to thank me for keeping an eye out for you.'

'I know you meant it kindly, Laurence—'

'Well, you might try sounding a little more friendly. Isn't that your boss over there?'

Gerald Hedwin had seen her and was coming across, a young, pretty girl on his arm. He introduced her as his daughter Nora, and there were general greetings, during which he studied her appearance with approval.

'You really do Orchid proud,' he said, beaming. 'I was a bit concerned when you were late. Might be our big night, you know. Pity if you weren't there.'

Laurence gave her a sidelong glance of triumph. Delia tried to be grateful, although she felt as though shackles were being hung onto her. But she smiled and said the right things. It was almost a relief when Brian hurried across with Mark trotting at his heels. They glanced hurriedly from herself to Mr Hedwin, trying to calculate what they'd missed.

'It's the clash of the Titans tonight,' Brian remarked jovially. 'Delia and Mark. Rumour says that it's between you two. Well, it's all good for Orchid.'

'I must confess to crossing my fingers for Delia,' Mr Hedwin said. 'Mark's entry is work he did outside, but hers was an Orchid campaign.'

'Yes, of course, of course.' Brian recovered himself hastily. 'Delia's campaign was excellent. I said so at the time when she asked my advice on a few little points…'

'Did I?' Delia asked pointedly. 'I think you were on vacation, and didn't return until it was all done.'

'Oh, yes, but we wrapped it up together. I'm sure you recall that.'

Mr Hedwin's eyes gleamed with malicious enjoyment at this exchange. He stopped a passing waiter and handed glasses around. 'Here's to both of you,' he said. 'And may the best person win.'

As they threaded their way to the table Laurence murmured, 'It looks like you've got it in the bag.'

'What do you mean?'

'That was a damage-limitation exercise going on back there. Didn't you realise?'

She hadn't, but now it was obvious. Brian thought she'd won and had been trying to claim a share of her glory. Delia took a deep breath and forced herself to concentrate on what was happening now. She'd dreamed of moments like this.

The room was dominated by a raised dais on which stood a long table for the guests of honour. Behind it was a huge blow-up of the statuette that was given to each award winner.

Circular tables filled the body of the room, with eight places at each. Delia knew most of her companions, at least slightly. The dinner was excellent, the talk good, and she found the others giving her glances of appraisal. After the toasts the president of the society rose to start the ceremony.

After a few minor awards the president beamed and said, 'And now for that part of the contest that is most eagerly awaited every year. Youth is the lifeblood of our profession, and the spotting of new talent is one of the...'

Brian was looking at Delia anxiously from his nearby table. Mark was drumming his fingers on the table.

'...seven campaigns entered, all of them excellent...'

Delia tried to let nothing show in her expression.

'...very hard decision...'

Mr Hedwin was looking at the ceiling in apparent unconcern.

'By a unanimous vote, the winner was—*Ms Delia Summers for her excellent promotion of Vital by Orchid.*'

Applause washed over Delia as she rose and made her way up the steps. She'd forgotten to prepare a speech, just in case, but suddenly her head was clear. She was aware of everything, including Mr Hedwin cheering, Brian clapping politely, but looking ready to spit feathers. Mark forced a smile, but appeared on the verge of tears.

The noise died away. 'Ladies and gentlemen, I can't tell you what this means to me, and I should like to thank...'

Once she'd begun it was easy to go on. She managed a couple of witticisms that drew genuine laugh-

ter, and praised Orchid products for 'being so good
that they promote themselves'. Light bulbs flashed,
and she returned to her seat amid applause. It was
over.

There were more awards. She sat through them
with an air of attentiveness, clapped and cheered in
the right places. But she was functioning on automatic.

'Come on, darling,' Laurence chivvied. 'You ought
to be dancing with joy.'

Only a few weeks ago she would have been. Once,
she'd have been delighted with that shiny statuette,
and the annoyance of Brian and Mark would have
been all part of an enjoyable game. But none of it
mattered beside the memory of a man who'd sent her
away when she longed only to be in his arms. What
did Craig think of her now? What would he tell
Alison if she called? Please, she thought, let the evening end soon!

When the award ceremony was finally over Nora
Hedwin approached their table, ostensibly to congratulate Delia, although her eyes constantly strayed
to Laurence's handsome profile. Her father asked
Delia for a dance. 'I'm proud of you,' he said as they
twirled the floor. 'It's good for the firm to have an
award winner, and I was impressed by your speech.'
His voice became confidential. 'Between you and me,
Brian's as sick as a parrot at your success. You know
what he's up to, don't you?'

'Trying to grease Mark into his job when he
leaves.'

'That's right. Of course, Mark is good, and maybe
he'll get the job, maybe he won't. I just thought you'd

like to know that I'm fully aware of the scheming, and I'm not entirely sold on Mark. Everything's still to play for.'

'Thank you for telling me,' Delia said politely.

What was Craig doing now? Could she slip away to call him?

'But you haven't sewn it up yet,' he continued. 'I've always been impressed by your commitment, Delia. First in the office, last out. Now you dash off at the first chance, and I often feel that your mind is elsewhere.'

'But surely my work hasn't suffered?' she asked quickly. 'I work right through lunch.'

'Yes, but you're playing into Mark's hands if he's there and you aren't. Still, enough of that. I know I only have to drop a hint. Now let's enjoy ourselves.'

Delia smiled brightly and said something appropriate. After that she had to dance with Brian, and listen to his insincere compliments. Mark followed, and his efforts to cover his chagrin provided some light relief.

'I'm delighted for you to have your little moment of glory,' he purred.

'But you'd have been even more delighted to have it yourself?' she said sweetly.

'My dear girl, I only entered to make up the numbers. They were pitifully small in that category. Which rather takes the gilt off the gingerbread, but I don't want to spoil your night.'

'On the contrary, you're making my night,' she assured him. 'Don't be spiteful, Mark. It suits you only too well.'

His lips tightened, but he was too wise to challenge her further.

Laurence was missing when she returned to the table, and she saw him dancing smoochily with Nora. Delia couldn't blame him. The girl's blatant admiration must have come as sweet balm after her own awkwardness. She had another coffee and refused further invitations to dance.

Laurence returned, full of apologies for his 'neglect', and she smiled warmly. After all, she owed him something for protecting her interests.

'It's done you good to get out,' he observed. 'I don't know how you stand it cooped up with the cripple.'

Delia stiffened. '*What* did you say?'

'All right, all right. One isn't supposed to say crippled. Visually challenged. Blind as a bat. What's the difference? He's still leeching on you.'

'How dare you say such a thing?' Delia flashed. 'Craig isn't a cripple. He spends his life fighting not to depend on people—'

'Oh, yes? That's why you're in his house, is it?'

'I'm there because I chose to be. I forced him to accept me for his little girl's sake. Craig is a strong, independent man and—and ten times the man you are.'

'Oh, come on, darling! Defending him's one thing, but that's going a bit far, isn't it? If you ask me, he's making the most of the situation.'

'What do you mean by that?'

'Having you around, attending to his every whim. I wouldn't mind a gorgeous handmaid, I can tell you.'

'You're incurably vulgar, Laurence. As for my being gorgeous—he's blind.'

'He knows you're a looker, though. He told me.'

'*What*? What did he say?'

'Oh—some nonsense!'

'What did he say?' Delia asked in agony. 'Tell me. I must know.'

'I told him how much it mattered to you to get on in the world, and he started on about how I was doing you an injustice. He said underneath was the real Delia—gentle and beautiful—or something like that. I can't remember. Hey, where are you going?'

Delia had risen quickly and gathered up her things. 'Goodnight, Laurence. Thank you for bringing me; I'm sorry I can't stay any longer. And please take this back.' She unclasped the ruby necklace. 'It was kind of you, but I can't accept it. No, don't come with me. I'll get a taxi.'

'But you can't just dash off like— What about this?' Laurence held up her award, but he was talking to empty air.

CHAPTER TEN

EXCEPT for the lamp over the front door, the house was dark when Delia let herself in. She could hear nothing. Craig must have gone to bed. It was a relief not to have to face him, yet it would have been nice if he'd waited up for her.

She climbed the stairs, moving quietly so as not to disturb him. But her way led past the door of his bedroom, standing open, and she sensed a faint movement within. She glanced inside.

The curtains were drawn back and there was a little light from the window, by which she could just make out Craig. He was sitting on the bed with his head bent, his face buried in the silk scarf Delia had worn earlier that day. He looked like a man seeking refuge.

She was shocked by the sight of him. Before, she'd known only Craig's strength—all he'd allowed her to know. But now his defences were down because he thought there was no one to see him.

He raised his head, and she nearly cried out at the sight of his ravaged face. There was the truth that he hid from the world. Beneath the efficiency and cool irony he was tortured to the point of madness. But was it only his blindness, or was there something more? The compulsive movement of his fingers in her scarf, the way he held it to his face, inhaling her perfume, suggested another possibility, one that made Delia's heart leap. If only…

But then he crumpled the scarf and tossed it aside. He buried his head in his hands, tearing at his hair like a man possessed, while a groan broke from the depths of him.

'Craig,' she said softly. 'Craig—don't. There's no need.'

His head jerked up at the sound of her voice. His face was full of horror. He would have risen from the bed, but Delia went to him, dropping down on one knee and taking his face between her hands. He grew very still.

'Why?' she asked him urgently. 'Why this?'

'You should have told me,' he said fiercely. 'Damn you! Why couldn't you have been honest with me?'

'I don't know what you mean.'

'I mean this little game you've been playing. It looks like kindness, but it's actually the worst kind of cruelty. Be nice to the poor sightless fool. Make him think he means something to you. Then go away feeling like Lady Bountiful.

'Or is it worse than that? Did you set out to drive me crazy? Does it make you feel good to know that I can't stop thinking about you, night or day? I can't work properly because I'm wondering about you. When you're there I want to know if you're looking at me, and what you think of what you see.

'I had to be your fool, didn't I, like all the others? It was just a test of technique. I can't be impressed with your more obvious assets, so I was a harder nut to crack. What a challenge! But you rose to it, triumphantly.'

'Stop it,' she cried in anguish. 'How dare you speak

to me like that? What have I done to deserve it? I didn't want to go out. You forced me to.'

'I hope you had an enjoyable time,' he said stiffly.

'No, I had a rotten time. I was thinking about you.'

'You mean worrying about me, don't you? Like Alison?'

'Craig, what's happened to you? You were so different before—I felt we were really getting close—'

'Close?' he echoed derisively. 'How close can we be when you're in love with another man?'

'I'm not in love with any other man.'

'Maybe you don't have to be in love with him to live with him. Or is it one of those modern arrangements where you each have the key to the other's flat? It makes no difference. You should have told me the situation between you and that man. I suspected something when he called you that first night, but not this.'

'The ''situation'' between Laurence and me is that he's my ''ex''—insofar as he was ever anything. But he doesn't have a key to my flat, and never did.'

'Yet he managed to get in and go through your wardrobe.'

Light dawned. 'Oh, Craig, you fool.' She could hardly keep the laughter out of her voice. It was laughter of relief and joy as much as amusement.

'Don't laugh at me, damn you! *Don't laugh.*'

'I'm not really. Craig, I swear I don't love Laurence. I live alone, but just now I've got a friend staying with me. She let him in.'

He was tense, like a man who feared to believe good news, lest he wake and find it a dream. 'He knew what dress to go for,' he said warily.

'He's seen me in it before. It's vulgar. I didn't mind

that then but I do now. It's all over between him and
me. There never was very much, and he met a girl
tonight who really admires him. Craig, please forget
about Laurence.'

'If only I could,' he murmured longingly.

'You must. He isn't between us. You're the one
I—the one I love.' It took all her courage to utter the
words.

'Don't say that if it isn't true,' he said hoarsely.

'It *is* true. I don't know when it began. Somehow
it just happened. By the time I realised, it was too
late.' She tried to read his face, but it showed nothing,
and her heart sank. 'If you don't love me...' she began in a faltering voice.

She got no further. His arms tightened around her,
crushing her against him, and his mouth was on hers.
He kissed her urgently, seeking the answers to questions he couldn't ask. She gave him those answers
with all her heart. At last he was casting away his
barriers of suspicion, revealing himself to her, in a
way she'd hardly dared hope for.

She knew now why her heart had been cool for so
many years. She'd been waiting to meet the one man
who could set it on fire. Now it had happened and her
life was beginning. She gave herself up to him freely,
gladly, wanting only to be his.

His lips moved insistently on hers. His hands roved
over her, seeking out her shape. The feel of her slender body inflamed him. The tight dress lovingly
emphasised every curve and valley, exciting his imagination.

'I was sure you were his,' he murmured. 'I
wouldn't let myself think of you—'

'I've thought about you from the first moment. I tried not to. I disliked you, but I couldn't get you out of my mind.' The last words were muffled as she laid her lips once more against his.

He seemed to hesitate, as though waiting to know what he should read into this. But her soft mouth was persuasive, sending him messages he couldn't ignore. 'Craig,' she whispered. 'Craig…'

'Is this what you want?' he asked, drawing her closer.

'Yes,' she whispered. 'This is what I want…'

He burned as if with fever. There was hunger in his embraces. 'Don't do this unless you mean it,' he begged.

Delia slipped her hand behind her back and pulled down the zip that held the skin-tight dress in place. He heard the soft rasping sound, felt her rise to her feet, taking his hands and placing them on the dress. A slight pull and it slipped down easily. Her slip followed and soon there was nothing between his eager hands and her naked body. He sighed, burying his face against her flesh, inhaling its sweet aroma of womanly warmth and desire. Then her heart was beating wildly close to his ear, and the sound gave him courage to take the next step into the strange, mysterious world that her love promised.

He rose to face her, enjoying her soft movements as she peeled away his clothes. He half feared the moment of nakedness, when she would have the advantage of sight, but it was gone in an instant. It felt right to discard all barriers, and free their mutual passion.

He took her in his arms gently, thrilling to the feel

of her skin against his own. He'd once thought he could guess how she looked, but she was a revelation, more delicately built than he'd imagined. Her breasts were small and rounded, each one fitting his cupped hand as if made for it. Against his own size and strength she was almost lost, and a new feeling of protectiveness filled him as he slowly drew her down on the bed beside him.

Delia gave herself up to his caresses gladly, but with a feeling almost of awe. She'd craved this moment, but now that it was here she had no idea where it would lead. With every tender touch he took her further into a new dimension, where she could forget herself. Her insides seemed to dissolve, no longer flesh but pure sensation, where every feeling evoked its opposite. There was joy, but it was of the bittersweet kind, and hope blended with fear. Alongside an adventurous longing to explore these new realms was an instinct to hurry back to the safety she'd once known.

But it was too late for that. She no longer knew herself. The once proud woman had turned into someone who would put her hand gladly into her lover's and say, 'Lead me.'

His embrace grew stronger, as if he'd discovered what he needed to know, and all was well. The darkness was no hindrance to him now. He could claim the woman his heart desired as much as his flesh without fear, because with every touch, every softly whispered word she told him how willingly she made the gift.

At the moment of their perfect union he felt flooded by a kind of peace that he hadn't known for seven years. The world was a new place where everything was possible, because she loved him.

At last Delia felt herself become completely his, as she'd longed to be. To her wonder and delight it was everything she'd dreamed of. His prickly shell had been discarded and he gave himself to her as totally as he claimed her. And he gave everything, not merely his passion but also his pain and his need. He wanted more than her love. He wanted her comfort. He would never ask for it in words, because he couldn't. But he could entreat it in the urgency of his kiss, in the way his arms enfolded her body, as though protecting a long-lost treasure. Most of all, he told her what she needed to know when he finally fell asleep with his head on her breast.

Slowly Delia opened her eyes. But her blissful smile faded at the sight of Craig, sitting on the edge of the bed, his head buried in his hands.

'Craig?'

He reached out for her, but his head was still bent. 'What is it?' she asked in dismay. 'What's wrong?'

'I had no right to do that,' he groaned. 'I swore that I wouldn't—and yet—' He could say no more. Somehow his peace had deserted him. It might still be there, somewhere, but it was a new-born infant that must be constantly nourished to survive. When he'd found himself alone again in his own head he'd realised that the path was still rocky.

'You swore not to make love to me?' Delia echoed. 'Why?'

'Because I'm the man I am. What chance would we have?'

She pulled herself up in bed and threw her arms around him. 'The chance we give ourselves. If we love each other anything is possible.'

'Do you want to hear me say I love you?' he asked gruffly. 'All right, I'll say it. I love you. I love everything about you. Not just your beauty, but your honesty and courage, and your compassion.' He gave a brief, self-mocking laugh. 'Another good resolution gone.'

'If you resolved not to love me, that was a *bad* resolution,' Delia said strongly.

'And what can I offer you? A life shackled to a man who's full of demons and suspicion, who's likely to yell at you because sometimes he—just—can't—cope.' He said the last words with his hands clenched.

'But you do a great job of coping,' she said, pleadingly.

'Only on the outside. Inside—' He checked himself, on the verge of revealing to her what he'd never discussed with another living soul.

'Inside, you have only the darkness,' she said softly.

He reached for her, startled by the precision with which she'd voiced his thought. The sighted didn't understand that when you were blind the darkness was everywhere, not just in your eyes. But *she* knew.

At last he relaxed enough to lean back against the pillows, one arm behind his head, the other holding her close. 'I wish we'd met years ago,' he said, 'when I was a real man.'

'I have no complaints on that score,' Delia murmured demurely, and he gave a crack of laughter.

'Thank you, but that wasn't what I meant. When I

had my eyes I was a *man*. I was in charge. I could go out and make the world dance to my tune.'

'You don't do so badly now,' she observed. 'But I'd love to know what you were like in those days.'

'I expect my sister told you about our family. You had to achieve. Nothing else counted. It can be tough on a child, and I've never pressurised Alison that way. But I thrived on it.'

'I can imagine,' she said, nestling against him and dropping a tender kiss on his chest. 'Go on.'

'I felt like a king. I made a success of business, married a woman all the other men had wanted and we had a wonderful baby. Everything worked out as I'd planned. I was in control. And then—' a shudder went through him '—I discovered that my control was an illusion. One fall, and it was all taken away from me. I was left groping about helplessly in the dark— an object of derision, most of all to myself.'

'Derision?' she said, aghast. 'Surely people didn't—?'

'Some hid it better than others. Gillian, my mother-in-law, always disliked me. She thought me aggressive and bumptious, which I suppose I was. She fought me for custody of Alison. She said a "helpless man" had no right to raise her grandchild. Luckily the court found my wife's lover as disgusting as I did, and when they learned that he was always welcome in Gillian's house—in fact she'd introduced them— they let me keep Alison. But I've tried to keep contact with my in-laws for Alison's sake, and to be a normal father to her, and not accept her help more than I have to.'

'For her sake—or yours?' Delia asked gently.

'For hers of course. Well, perhaps a little for mine too. I feel uneasy when she mothers me. And it isn't fair to Alison.'

'Is it fair to her to reject her love?'

'I never reject her love.'

'Perhaps you don't mean to, but I think it comes across to her like that. She enjoys looking after you. She loves you terribly, Craig, and that's how she shows it. And when you reject her care you hurt her.'

'I'm just trying to give her a little normal, childhood freedom.'

'Of course, but don't push her away. I've seen her expression when she's doing something for you.'

'So have I. It's in her voice: very kind and wise, like a nanny.'

'Maybe you're not listening closely enough. You haven't picked up her happiness when she feels necessary to you. It's Alison's nature to care. She'll probably become a doctor, or one of those lawyers who only ever work for the defence. Anything where she can help people. If only you could tell her sometimes that you need her.'

He didn't answer this, but his grip on her hand tightened, and Delia understood. From the start he'd felt his blindness as a humiliation, and had fought to prove himself as good a man as any other.

But he'd overdeveloped one side of himself—the tough, need-nobody side—while his capacity for tenderness was in danger of withering because he was afraid to show it. Even their love was something he'd felt as a weakness, and not yielding to weakness was important to him. There were so few parts of his life where he felt in control.

'Never mind that now,' she said, drawing him close. 'We have so much to learn about each other. And it's Sunday. We don't have to go into work...'

They spent the day loving and talking. He insisted on doing the cooking, but now it was different. He was no longer proving himself, but performing a loving service for his lady. For the first time she heard him give a full-bodied laugh. He could even make jokes.

'You've given me a real problem,' he said as they lay together on Sunday evening. 'What am I going to do about Alexandra?'

'Your personal assistant—sorry, secretary?'

'The very one. She stayed in the north on purpose so that I'd be without her at the meeting. It's her way of showing me how much I need her, so that I'll promote her. I won't stand for blackmail, so I was going to fire her.'

'But?'

'If she hadn't let me down you wouldn't have come with me, and we might not have discovered each other in time.'

'In time?'

'Soon it might have been too late for me. My defences were growing every day.'

'It doesn't make any difference,' she promised. 'No matter how thick they grew I'd have found a way in, less for your sake than for mine. I need you so much.'

'You—need me?'

'You're the only man who's ever seen me properly.'

This time he didn't ask what she meant, but held

her tightly. At last he said, 'So I really owe Alexandra a debt of gratitude.'

'What are you going to do?'

He grinned. 'I think I'll promote her instead—for services rendered. Delia, my love...'

But as she was snuggling up to him blissfully the phone rang. 'Alison,' they announced together.

'I adore my daughter,' Craig said, groaning, 'but she has a lousy sense of timing.' He lifted the bedside receiver and said, 'Hello, darling?'

Delia could hear Alison's voice clearly as she asked the question that was always top of her list.

'I'm fine,' Craig said instinctively, but then added quickly, 'Except for missing you.'

Alison sounded anxious. 'Isn't Miss Summers looking after you properly?'

'Yes—of course she is—but—' Craig signalled to Delia wildly for help. She placed her hand over the mouthpiece and whispered, 'But it's not the same as having my girl.'

Craig repeated the words, hoping Alison hadn't heard enough to be suspicious. Instead her voice was filled with almost painful eagerness as she asked. 'Do you really miss me, Daddy?'

'More than you'll ever know, darling. Especially at breakfast, when you usually read bits out of the paper to me. And in the evening, when you usually come dashing in—and the daft programmes you watch on TV, and—' Delia whispered again '—the way you kiss me goodnight, and so many things.'

'Do you want me to come home?'

'Don't you dare. You stay and enjoy yourself. I just

want you to know that I'm thinking about you, all the time.'

Delia slipped away. Craig needed to talk to his daughter alone, and tell her what was in his heart, if he could. It might be too much to ask, all at once, but he'd made a start.

Without her, Craig found that the words were harder, but he was touched by Alison's eager question. 'Do you really miss me, Daddy? Really and truly?'

'Really and truly,' he promised. The ecstatic little sigh that reached him down the phone line was a revelation. It meant that much to her! And he hadn't known.

He tried again. He was awkward, but she drank up every encouraging word like a desert thirsting for a few drops of water. By the time they hung up Alison was completely happy. Craig lay there, feeling guilty that he'd been too self-absorbed to read his daughter's heart.

But it wasn't too late. Truly Delia had come to him 'in time'. But perhaps only just.

He called her name, wanting to reach out to her in passionate gratitude, and suddenly she was there beside him, in his arms.

CHAPTER ELEVEN

ON THE night before Alison was due back Craig arrived home early and set himself to make a special supper for Delia. He had a new recipe and wanted to surprise her.

The last week had been the happiest of his life, not just in the years since his blindness, but of his whole life. He'd thought himself happy when he'd married Philippa, but looking back he recognised that he'd always known something was amiss, that one day she would coolly betray him. Now, looking into Delia's heart, he knew he'd found the perfect woman: warm, loving, and with a pure truth of the heart that would never fail him.

He'd prided himself on his inner eye, which he'd believed saw everything. But Delia had shown him the things he'd missed in his spiritual blindness. She'd seen the danger with Alison, and taught him how to avoid it. For that she would have not only his love but also his eternal gratitude.

She'd also revealed to him the danger within himself, the subtle twisting that bitterness that had caused in his character. In her arms he'd felt his nature become straight again. Bitterness was something that could be conquered, because she was there.

He smiled as he found himself thinking of Philippa as his *first* wife, which meant that he was planning a second. But, while his subconscious had decided that he must marry Delia, his reason drew back.

To him their love represented risk. He was used to an ordered world where things were always in the same place. Now this woman who was like no other had invited him to step into the unknown with her. In that new place nothing would be familiar, but infinite joy would reward the brave man.

But was he a brave man? He'd never doubted it before. His steely courage had brought him through hell. Now, faced with the ultimate challenge, he was uncertain. Suddenly nothing was in its familiar place.

He'd talked it all over with himself many times, trying to be sensible. But how could a man be sensible with the memory of her lips and hands, and the generous outpourings of her heart? Every day his doubts grew fainter. Perhaps this very evening, when he was holding her hand and picturing how she looked in the candlelight...

The phone rang when he was at an awkward moment in the cooking. Craig cursed, and turned the gas down before he answered.

'Hello?'

'I have to talk to Delia urgently,' came Laurence's brusque voice.

'She's not here. Can I get her to call you back?'

'When will she be in? This is important.'

'I'm expecting her in about half an hour,' Craig said, trying not to be annoyed by the other man's rudeness.

'Tell her to call me at once. *At once*. Are you sure you understood that?'

'Quite sure,' Craig said coldly. 'I'm blind, not brain-dead.'

'Well, I sure as hell don't know where your wits have been wandering recently,' Laurence snapped. 'You have a lot to answer for.'

'Perhaps you'd like to tell me what that means?'

'She's lost that job. It's going to Mark Gorham. I told her this would happen if she wasted her time on you. She should have been in there fighting, not letting it go by default. Now it's too late. I hope you're pleased with yourself.'

'Have you finished?' Craig asked in an iron-hard voice.

'I'll just say this. Delia was wide awake before you got your claws into her, making her feel guilty. Why the hell should she throw her life away on your problems? Just tell her to call me.' Laurence hung up.

Delia arrived back half an hour later, to find Craig on the leather sofa, his head thrown back. She leaned down and kissed him, but he barely responded.

'There was a message for you to call Laurence,' he said.

'Laurence? But that's all over.' Delia laughed. 'And I know he's not pining for me because he consoled himself pretty fast with Nora Hedwin.'

'Just call him,' Craig said.

Laurence answered at once. 'What's up, Laurence?'

'I warned you that you'd lose that job if you weren't careful, but would you listen?'

'Mr Hedwin is still considering—'

'That's what you think. Mark has been privately told that it's his. Nora told me.'

Delia turned so that she had her back to Craig, and

spoke in a low voice. 'How certain is Nora about this?'

'Dead certain. I'd say you had only yourself to blame, but I think the real blame lies elsewhere—'

'That's enough,' she said quietly. 'Thank you for letting me know.' She hung up, feeling as if she'd had a blow in the stomach. Laurence had warned her. Craig had warned her. Now it had happened, and the injustice hurt. Not as much as it once would have done, but it hurt.

She looked at him, lying with his head back against the sofa, and a fierce urge to protect him made her resolve to keep silent. She put her head up and walked over to him.

'Well?' Craig asked.

'Nothing much,' she said cheerfully. 'Just Laurence making a fuss about trivia, as usual.'

'I wouldn't call it nothing that Mark has stabbed you in the back over that job.'

Delia drew in her breath. She'd been too upset to consider what Laurence might have told Craig.

'I only meant that it's not important,' she said lightly.

'Not important?' There was a warning note in Craig's voice.

'Not the end of the world. There are other jobs.'

'But you wanted this one. And you've lost it. And you didn't tell me. And I know why. You were being "kind". Don't tell the blind man the damage he's done in case he feels useless—or worse.'

'No,' she said frantically. 'It wasn't like that. What did Laurence say to you?'

'Only the truth—that I destroyed your chances.'

'You didn't. Mark and Brian just intrigued too cleverly—'

'And you let them get away with it. Why the devil did you take the risk?'

'Because I love you,' she said passionately. 'Because I wanted to be with you more than anything else—'

'Because you wanted to *look after* me,' he interrupted. 'You're very generous.'

Delia took a sharp breath. 'If you don't know the difference between love and pity then our time together has been wasted. Didn't it mean anything to you?'

'You'll never know how much it meant,' he said harshly. 'But I've been living in a fool's paradise. I batten on people and destroy their lives. I try not to, but it happens anyway. Alison, and now you. I damage everyone, and I can't take that any more.'

'Craig, please,' she cried frantically. She could see her new-found happiness slipping away, and she was terrified that she couldn't stop it. 'Can't you understand what you've done for me? You made me believe that I have some value, apart from my looks. For the first time in my life I feel worth something. Not my face, *me*. And you did that.'

'Then I'm glad. At least I gave you something good to set against the harm. But I won't let you risk yourself for me again.'

'Whether I get this job or not doesn't matter, not like it used to—'

'But it *will* matter again, and very soon. What will be in your eyes then, Delia, that I'll never see? This man lost me everything, because he's maimed and useless. I threw my chances away for him, and he selfishly let me.'

'*No!*' she cried.

'Do you think I could endure life wondering what you're thinking, tortured because I can't see your feelings in your eyes?'

'What about last night?' she burst out. 'And the other nights when we lay together in the darkness— you couldn't see me then, and I couldn't see you. But you didn't need sight to know my heart. If you don't know by now that I love you—if you don't love me—'

'You don't need to ask me that,' he said. 'Yes, I love you—enough to send you away before my blindness ruins your life.'

'It doesn't matter,' she cried. 'It's you I love, what you *are*. I can't leave you—don't ask me to. We could have so much...'

He found his way towards her, and took hold of her arms, firmly but gently. 'But we couldn't.' he said. 'The poison is in me. If I were a better man, perhaps I could overcome it. For a while I thought I had. But the reality is always there, waiting to catch us. Whatever we could have had is a ''might have been'', and it must stay that way.'

'Why have you so little faith in me?' she demanded in agony.

'Not in you. In myself. For both our sakes you should go at once.'

'No, I've got to be here when Alison gets home.'

'That's tomorrow. It's best if she knows nothing about this.'

'So we smile and shake hands as if nothing has

happened?' she asked, horrified. 'And we part "good friends"?'

His face was already withered with suffering. 'What else can we do?' he asked quietly.

The campers were returning by coach. Craig came with her to the coach station and they endured the journey in silence. It had all been said.

Alison jumped from the coach and flung herself against her father with an eagerness that made him gasp. They all laughed at that and the moment was eased. On the way home she chattered about the wonderful time she'd had.

Delia had her bags packed and was ready to leave at once, but Alison promptly vetoed this plan. 'I want to give you your present,' she said. 'Oh, you *must* wait.'

She'd bought Delia a charming print of wild flowers. Her gift to her father was a heavy piece of wood that she herself had whittled down into the rough shape of an owl. She guided his hands over it, indicating various features, letting him feel the varnish. Craig smiled and thanked her warmly. Delia watched them, glad that he'd at least managed to take this step, and even more glad that Alison suspected nothing.

But misery was clouding her perceptions, and she failed to notice Alison's quick glance between them.

At last she could get away. Alison had bounded upstairs to unpack, and Craig came with Delia to the car.

'Goodbye, Delia,' he said quietly.

'I can't believe it's going to end like this,' she whispered.

'Perhaps it hasn't. Maybe one day—maybe even soon—' He took a sharp breath as if dismayed at what he was saying.

'What do you mean by that, Craig?'

'Nothing. I'm talking nonsense.'

'You sound as if you hoped for something.'

'I tell you it was nothing,' he said angrily. 'I never hope. Hope just destroys you. Remember that.' He turned abruptly and went back into the house. Delia watched him go, wondering how anything could hurt so much and still leave her standing.

Delia expected to be given the bad news about the job at once, but day followed day and nothing happened except that Mark vanished and was seen no more. At last she received the summons and went to Mr Hedwin's office. Brian too was there, with a smile fixed on his face by sheer force.

'Congratulations,' Mr Hedwin said, extending his hand to her as soon as she appeared. 'You've just been appointed Orchid's new chief publicity director.' He added, slightly too firmly, 'Brian is as pleased as I am.'

'Delighted,' Brian murmured, his eyes glassy.

It appeared that he was to leave in two weeks' time, much earlier than Delia had expected. 'I should have retired last year, but Mr Hedwin particularly requested me to stay,' he explained loftily. 'But now my successor has been chosen I feel that the time has come to lay down the burdens.'

So Brian had stayed on to smooth Mark's path, and now that he'd failed he was jumping ship. He confirmed this indirectly as they returned to their own offices. 'I ought to congratulate you, my dear Delia, but I find I really can't do it,' he said spitefully.

'I understand how you feel, Brian.'

'I doubt that. Honest competition is one thing, but sneaking in by the back way is something I dislike.'

'Then why did you try to sneak Mark in by the back way? Was that honest competition?'

'It was a sight more honest than getting your friends to pull strings for you.'

Delia stared. 'Nobody pulled strings for me, Brian.'

'Oh, please, don't pretend you didn't know what was going on.'

'I thought Mark had got it—'

'He had, until you got Craig Locksley to go into action for you.'

Her heart lurched at the mention of Craig's name, but she was still puzzled. 'What has he got to do with this? He's not a member of the firm.'

'But he's very important to Orchid right now. When he told Hedwin that you were the only one he could deal with, it went a long way, as you knew it would.'

'I swear I didn't know—'

'Oh, please,' Brian interrupted disdainfully. 'I detest affectations of innocence. I just hope your victory doesn't turn sour in your mouth.'

'You mean you hope it does,' Delia replied with spirit.

He shrugged. 'Either way, we shall soon be out of each other's hair.'

He stalked off, closing his door sharply behind him. Delia was left trying to come to terms with the shattering discovery. Craig had intervened to help her. For a moment her heart glowed. He was thinking of her.

But, of course, he'd done it for the sake of his own pride. Some of her elation died as she recalled his bitterness at her loss, and how he'd blamed himself. Now he'd put things right. That was all there was to it.

Several times she almost called Craig to thank him, but drew back. When at last she dialled his work number, his secretary informed her that he was away for a few days. She called his home and heard his answering machine. Perhaps he'd taken a holiday with Alison. She never tried again. He'd dismissed her so finally, and this last gesture was merely tying up ends. He didn't want to hear from her.

The only other thread of contact she could maintain with him was the story of the child-labour firm. Craig had achieved everything he'd wanted. When the shares had gone into their final nosedive the board had given in and reversed its policy. The foreign factories were being closed down, and factories at home were re-opening. Leabridge and Derham had both announced early retirement, 'due to ill health', and departed without bonuses.

Brian was making her life as awkward as possible. Several times she asked him to talk to her and hand over the reins in an orderly manner. He promised, but the meetings were always delayed. Then, abruptly, he pronounced himself too ill to work further, and was never seen at Orchid again. So Delia was thrown in at the deep end, with no help from Brian at all. The files were full of things he'd concealed from her, and at first she was all at sea, as he'd obviously intended.

Luckily Brian's secretary was a tower of strength. Even so, Delia worked all hours, determined to succeed despite obstacles. She was first in the office and last out. On Saturday morning she went in until lunchtime, and when she left she was carrying a heap of files.

As she drove home her mind was racing with thoughts of the work she would do that afternoon. By day she always kept her mind running on something, to stop it lingering on Craig. That would come late at night, when she was alone in bed, and he could no longer be shut out. All the way up in the lift she was mentally drafting letters. But then the lift reached her floor, the doors opened, and Delia saw something that wiped all else from her mind.

'Alison!'

The child had been sitting beside Delia's front door. Now she jumped up eagerly and went straight into her arms. 'I'm so glad you've come,' she said in a muffled voice. 'I've been waiting and waiting. I was afraid I'd have to go without seeing you.'

There were a thousand questions to be asked, but Delia held them back until they were inside. Alison looked pale and unhappy.

'What is it?' Delia asked urgently. 'Is something wrong with your father? Did he send you?'

'No, Daddy doesn't know I'm here. I told him I wanted to get in touch with you, and he said not if I knew what was good for me.'

Delia sighed. How like the old Craig that sounded! 'But you came anyway?'

'Yes, because I may not know what's good for me, but I *do* know what's good for Daddy. Much better than he does.' Alison paused as though trying to summon up courage, took a deep breath and said, 'Miss Summers, are you and Daddy in love?'

'Yes, we are,' Delia said simply.

Alison sighed, as though the difficult part had been accomplished. 'I thought so. When I came home you were barely speaking to each other. The air was absolutely *jagged*,' she said dramatically. 'People don't get like that unless they mind terribly about each other.'

Delia gave a wan smile. 'Terribly,' she said. 'At least, I do. I thought he did too, but then he sent me away.'

Alison nodded. 'Daddy can be awfully silly sometimes,' she confirmed.

'He was convinced it was his fault I lost my promotion. But I got it anyway. It seems he had something to do with that.'

'I thought so,' Alison said wisely. 'I knew I had to get here somehow. I asked Grandma to bring me, but she said, "Nonsense," so I'm afraid I had to tell her a whopper. She thinks I'm at the cinema with a friend.'

Delia steered her into the kitchen and put on the kettle. 'Your grandmother? Is she staying with you?'

'Yes. I hate it.'

'I thought you liked her. Didn't you stay with her a while back?'

'That's my other granny: Daddy's mother. This is Grandma Gillian, and she's always cross because the court gave me to Daddy. She keeps making little barbed remarks about him not being able to look after me properly, but he *does*. I'm stuck with her until he gets out of hospital.'

'Oh, Alison, no! You mean he's ill?'

'Not ill. He's had an operation on his eyes. He's been trying to decide for weeks, and he made up his mind very suddenly.'

'You mean—he might be able to see again?' Delia could hardly get the words out.

'It's about a thirty per cent chance,' Alison said, sounding very knowledgeable. 'He's trying not to count on it.'

Pain and happiness warred within Delia. So much was happening to Craig, and she wasn't there to share it because he didn't want her. He'd sent her away because he wouldn't tie her to a blind man. If he regained his sight there might be hope for them. But he hadn't sought her help in his most crucial hour. Could any love survive that bitterness?

She began setting out cups, acting and speaking mechanically to cover her inner turmoil. 'Would you like something to eat?'

'Oh, please!' Alison said at once. 'Grandma's been taking lessons in nouvelle cuisine, and she's practising on me. Last night she served up something she said was soup, but it looked as though she'd just done the washing up in it. Honestly, sometimes I get desperate for egg and chips.'

'Egg and chips coming up!'

Slice the potatoes, she thought. Focus on them, think only of the food. Don't think that he doesn't want you. Heat up the chip pan. He doesn't even need you. Break the eggs. Concentrate. Maybe that will ease the pain.

'Why did he spend weeks deciding?' she asked at last. 'Why not jump at it at once?'

'I think it's because this is his one hope,' Alison said slowly. 'If it doesn't work, he'll have no hope left. That might be even harder than being blind.'

Delia nodded, accepting the child's opinion. Alison understood her father like no one else.

'This is smashing,' she said a few minutes later as she tucked into the food. 'I wish you were there instead of Grandma.'

'What about—?' Delia stopped delicately.

'My mother was just going on holiday,' Alison said woodenly.

'With Mr Elward?'

'No, he was over ages ago. It's Roy now—oh, no, he was last year. Now it's Joe—or somebody. I forget.'

'I see,' Delia said gently.

'It doesn't matter,' Alison said with a touch of defiance. 'I've got Daddy.' But then she added wistfully, 'I wish you two could have got it together. It would have been so nice.'

Delia squeezed her shoulder. 'Is there any news of Jenny?' she asked after a while.

'Oh, yes.' Alison brightened. 'We've got Jenny back, but she still can't go out in traffic, and I don't suppose she ever will now. If this operation doesn't work Daddy's going to need another guide dog. Jenny will just be a pet.'

'She'll hate that.'

'Oh, yes, she will,' Alison agreed at once. 'She's used to being really needed. She always looked so proud when her harness went on. She'll mind terribly if she's left behind while another dog does her work. I give her plenty of love to make her feel better.

Grandma says Jenny's getting old and it would happen anyway. But that's different.'

'Yes, that's honourable retirement,' Delia agreed. 'Jenny's going to feel she's failed. Oh, Alison, I'm so sorry. This is all my fault!'

'Is it?'

'I knocked her down.'

'I'd forgotten that. You just seem like a friend now. I can talk to you like no one else. Much better than Grandma. Better than Daddy sometimes.'

'Your father isn't an easy man.'

'No,' Alison said with feeling, and they smiled at each other like conspirators.

'When did all this happen?'

'About a week after you left. Daddy was very, very quiet. And then he suddenly began talking about the operation, asking me what I thought. Then he said he'd talk to the doctor about it again. He even asked me to go to the doctor with him. He's never, ever done that before.'

'I'm glad you were there.'

'So am I. He thought about it for a few more days, and then he said, "All right. We'll give it a try." He went into hospital a week ago. He came through the operation terribly well.' But the next moment the child's strong façade cracked, and there were tears in her eyes. 'Oh, Miss Summers, you've got to visit him. You've simply got to.'

'Darling, I want to. But if he doesn't want me—'

'He does, I know he does, but he won't say so. He's lonely and unhappy and—and scared. He'd be cross if he heard me say that, but I know he is. I try and try, but he won't talk about the worst, even to

me, because he thinks I'm a child. He can't even have
Jenny in the hospital, so he's all alone in the dark—'
She dropped her knife and fork and rubbed her eyes,
while tears poured down her cheeks.

At once Delia took her in her arms and the little
girl sobbed unrestrainedly. 'I don't know what to do
for him. Please, you must come and help.'

Did she dare to do this? Her heart longed to see
Craig again, and wouldn't it be worth the risk? If she
could only tell him how much she loved him, surely
then he'd understand, and open his arms to her?

'All right, Alison. I'll come with you.'

CHAPTER TWELVE

WHEN they were in the hospital corridor, Alison said, 'You come into Daddy's room with me, and don't say anything just at first. I'll tell Daddy, and then—you'll see. Everything will be all right.' She almost skipped the last few feet.

Delia held her breath as Alison opened the door slowly and the room came into view. There was the foot of the bed, then the coverlet with one hand lying on it, the sheet, and then the whiteness of the pillow. She bit her lip, trying not to cry out her distress. Craig's eyes were covered in bandages, and what was visible of his face was very pale. But what really tore at Delia was his stillness. It spoke eloquently of dread and despair.

It took all her self-control not to rush forward and put her arms about him, but she knew that was the last thing she must do. She had no place here unless Craig himself wanted her.

Suddenly he turned his head on the pillow. 'Is someone there?'

'It's me, Daddy.' Alison hurried forward as he held out his arms to her.

Delia stayed where she was, her heart hammering. Suppose his sixth sense were to tell him she was in the room? But he was absorbed in his daughter.

'I've been listening for you,' he said. 'But I didn't hear you. I must have been asleep.'

'You should put your radio on, so that you don't sleep too much in the day,' Alison lectured him gravely. 'Otherwise you won't sleep at night.'

'I know.' He touched her face. 'You always have good advice for me.'

'And you never take it.'

'I will in future.'

'Promise?'

'Promise. Now tell me what you've been doing. How are you managing with Grandma?'

Alison cast a look at Delia, who put a finger over her lips. Not yet. Alison nodded and began to talk about the nouvelle cuisine. Craig managed to laugh. He held on tightly to his daughter.

Delia kept very still, longing to put her arms around the man she loved, and promise him that she would be there for ever. But she must be patient.

'What else?' Craig asked. 'Tell me everything.'

Alison took a deep breath. 'I went to see Miss Summers.'

Craig was very silent for a moment. 'Why did you do that?' he asked at last.

'I needed to. I can't talk to Grandma. She doesn't understand, and Miss Summers does.'

Craig seemed to relax. 'If you did it for yourself, that's all right. Is she well, enjoying her new job?' He might have been asking about a stranger.

'She's working terribly hard, even on Saturdays.'

'Well, it's nice that she got what she wanted.'

'But she didn't,' Alison said, pleadingly. 'She wants you. You know she does. Just like you want—'

'That's enough,' he said sternly. 'There are some things we can't discuss. I suppose you told her about this?' He indicated his bandages. 'I wish you hadn't, but knowing you I'm sure you did.'

'Yes, and she wants to come and visit you.'

'Of course she does. She's a nice, kind person, but I—well, let's just say it's not a good idea. You can tell her I'm fine, but don't want any visitors—except you.' His arms tightened in a convulsive hug. '*You* stay with me,' he said, almost fiercely. 'I need you.'

Alison snuggled up to him, her face blissful. Delia watched them sadly. She knew she'd achieved something for the two people she loved. With her help they'd found each other. But there was no place for her. She backed quietly out of the room.

Because Alison kept in touch Delia was able to follow everything that happened to Craig. She knew the day he went home from hospital, still wearing bandages.

'The doctor wasn't keen but Daddy was desperate to be home,' Alison told her, having dropped in for a chat the day after Craig arrived home. 'So the doctor said yes, as long as he had a nurse.'

'What's the nurse like?'

'Not too bad. Her name's Vera. She tried to order Jenny off the bed at first, but Daddy said that was where Jenny belonged, and Vera backed down. Grandma's going home tomorrow.'

'I expect your grandfather will be glad to have her back.'

'Actually he said she should stay as long as she felt she was needed.' Alison gave a giggle. 'I don't think he likes drinking washing-up water either.'

'Is Jenny any better?'

Alison shook her head. 'But it doesn't matter just

now. Daddy likes to have her with him all the time. I play with her in the garden, but when the game's finished she goes straight back to him.'

'And what about you?'

Alison's smile told Delia what she wanted to know. 'He talks to me more now,' Alison said simply.

Delia smiled warmly, but her exclusion was very painful. Craig had found the way to reach out to his daughter, and his need of Jenny was greater than ever. But he refused to turn to the woman who loved him. She was shut out, pressing her face against the glass.

Day followed day, with no word from him. When he'd been home a week Delia could stand it no longer. One night, at about eleven o'clock, she got into her car and drove over to his house, parking some distance away. She walked back, entering his drive quietly, and going to a place under the trees, from which she could look up at his window.

She heard a rustling from the bushes and she stepped back. But it was only Jenny, having her final outing before going to bed. She stood still, sniffing the air, then turned and trotted over to Delia. She dropped to her knees, petting the dog, who received her embraces willingly.

'You remember me, don't you?' Delia said, and felt the rasp of Jenny's tongue in confirmation.

'How is he?' she whispered. 'Does he ever talk to you about me? Are you helping him to cope? Oh, why can't you speak?' She hugged Jenny fiercely, as Craig hugged her, trying to reach him just a little.

Then she heard the front door opening. Before she could back away Craig himself came out onto the step. In the dim light from the porch lamp she could just see that he was in pyjamas and dressing gown, with bandages over his eyes.

'Jenny,' he called.

The dog hurried over to him and he bent to pat her. 'Why were you so long, old girl?' he asked gently. 'Didn't you know I missed you?'

Suddenly he straightened up, all his senses alert. Delia held her breath, wondering if she dared reveal herself. Would it really do harm if she stepped forward and called his name? Wouldn't he be glad, after all?

'Is anyone there?' he called. Jenny gave a soft whine. 'What is it, girl? Is there someone?'

He listened again. Delia stayed silent. Her heart was aching, but the risk was too great.

Then he did something that almost broke her resolve. He leaned against the doorpost as if whatever was supporting him had suddenly given way. For a moment he dropped his face into his hands. Jenny pawed at him, whimpering. At last he straightened up and patted her.

'Come on, Jenny,' he said softly. 'Let's go inside and get to bed.'

Alison, in a dressing gown, was waiting for him at the top of the stairs. 'Are you all right, Daddy?'

'What are you doing out of bed at this hour?'

'I just came to make sure you were safely in.'

He touched her shoulder, smiling. 'You're like a mother hen with an awkward chick.'

'Someone needs to mother-hen you,' she said wisely. 'You look terrible. Let me see you safely in bed.'

Once he would have told her sharply that he needed

no help. But his heart understood more now, and he simply said, 'Thank you, darling.'

She settled him and pulled the bedclothes up with difficulty, since Jenny was already in position.

'Shove over,' Craig ordered her. 'This is my bed too.'

Jenny moved half an inch. Craig waited until his daughter had kissed him and departed before he wrapped an arm around the dog. 'You felt it, didn't you?' he murmured to her. 'So did I. But we were both wrong.'

Standing below, Delia saw the light in his room go off. Now she knew he was alone up there with his terrible private darkness, clinging onto his last hope. But not needing her. She stayed motionless, watching the window, for an hour. Then she went home.

Two days to go before the bandages came off. One day. On the evening before, Alison rang.

'The doctor's coming at eleven o'clock tomorrow morning,' she said. 'Daddy said he wanted it to happen at home. I'll call you straight after. Or perhaps—perhaps Daddy will.'

'Perhaps,' Delia said, trying to believe it.

She couldn't concentrate on her work. Her mind was with Craig, knowing that this day would bring the fulfilment of his dreams or the dashing of his last hope. And with it would go every last hope of her own.

But hadn't her hope already died? If Craig asked her back into his life only because he'd regained his sight it would only be second-best. She would return to him, because she loved him too much to refuse.

But the knowledge that he'd chosen to go through his crisis without her would always be there, poisoning what ought to be beautiful. They would share a crippled love, with something permanently missing. And how long could it last?

She couldn't help counting the hours. All of life had become focused on the approaching moment.

'Aren't you going to bed?' Maggie eventually asked.

'I will in a minute.'

'You've said that twice before. You can't sit watching that clock all night.'

When Maggie had gone to bed Delia tried to read a book, but the words danced. What was he doing now? Could he manage to sleep? Or was he lying awake, listening to the ticking of the clock, knowing that in a few hours his life would begin—or end?

The shrill of the phone brought her sharply upright. She snatched up the receiver. 'Hello?'

'Delia?' said the voice she'd feared never to hear again.

'*Craig,*' she whispered.

He sounded different. All the confidence had gone from his voice. 'You don't mind my calling you so late?'

'No—no, I'm glad you did. How are you?'

'Not so good. There are things that—well, I gather Alison's told you.'

'You mustn't be angry with her,' Delia said quickly.

'I'm not. I thought—you'll laugh at this, but I even thought you might come to me.'

'I wanted to, but you made it clear that you didn't need me.'

'I've needed you every moment since you went away. There hasn't been a time when I wasn't thinking of you, longing for you. And now more than ever—' His voice shook. 'Come now, Delia,' he said huskily. 'Come to me tonight. I can't stand it alone. I'm—afraid.'

'Wait for me,' she said breathlessly. 'I'm coming.'

She was out of the house in seconds. When she pulled into his drive she could already see Craig standing at the door, listening with painful eagerness. Another moment and she was in his arms.

'I was afraid you wouldn't come,' he said against her mouth. 'After I drove you away I thought there was no hope.'

'I never really went away,' she said. 'In my heart I was always with you. Kiss me, my love…kiss me…'

He responded fiercely. The feel of his lips on hers after the long, aching weeks was so good that she felt giddy. How could there be so much joy in the world?

He drew her inside, keeping his arms around her, as though afraid that she would vanish.

'You're really here, aren't you?' he asked urgently. 'You won't disappear?'

'I'm here for as long as you want me.'

'That'll be for ever. For ever and ever. I've thought so much about when the bandages come off tomorrow—if I can see you—and Alison. To live a normal life, with you as my wife—'

'And if you can't see, will you send me away again?' she asked.

'Never in this life,' he said fervently. 'I thought I

was strong enough to survive without you. But I'm not.'

'Craig, will you marry me? Will you promise to marry me whatever happens, in darkness or in light?'

'In darkness or in light,' he promised. 'In the darkness I'll need you more than ever. But while you're with me there will be no darkness.'

He led her to the top of the stairs and into his room. They discovered each other as lovers, but now everything was different. They'd been through the fire and learned that they couldn't survive apart. For him, especially, the discovery was like a flash of lightning over his black landscape, showing past and future. He knew that his future must be with her, whatever else might happen.

He made love to her like a man still trying to believe in his own blessings, half fearful of losing them, half triumphant that his faith had been justified. Other lovings had been full of passion. This one was full of tenderness as they consoled and reassured each other, not knowing if the day would bring heaven or hell, but ready for both, together.

Afterwards there was the warmth of his arms about her, and the infinite peace of lying together, knowing that they had come home to each other for ever.

While they lay together, there was a soft thump and the bed trembled as they were joined by a third presence that settled itself across Craig's legs. They both reached out and felt the silky fur. Two brown eyes gleamed in the darkness, watching them both contentedly, before closing. In minutes all three of them were asleep.

At dawn Delia awoke. Craig was lying with his arm

thrown over her, as though seeking refuge. Jenny had settled in the crook of his knees and was snoring. Delia kissed him and slid out of bed. In the closet she found a light dressing gown, and slipped it on so that she could sit at the window.

The darkness had turned to grey, and the scene outside was getting lighter by the moment. She thought of the coming day and what it would mean for so many people. If the worst came to the worst she wouldn't let Craig fall into the old melancholy pattern. She would use all her love and strength to make his life worth living.

For Alison it might mean a normal childhood at last, free of the responsibilities she'd assumed too young. But I'll make sure she has that anyway, Delia thought.

Even Jenny had something to lose or gain. If Craig could see again she would remain the only dog. If he couldn't, she'd suffer the heartbreak of becoming second-best.

It was seven o'clock. Delia realised that she must leave Craig's room. Alison would be up and about soon, and no doubt she would check on her father. She'd said she wanted Delia back, but how would she react to finding her here without warning?

But it was already too late. Even as Delia rose from the window seat the door handle turned and a small, tousled head appeared. It halted suddenly, and Alison's eyes met Delia's for a long moment, then a slow smile of delight crept over her features. Her face was full of a silent question. Delia nodded, returning her smile. Silently Alison put a finger over her lips and backed out of the room.

*   *   *

The doctor arrived at ten minutes to eleven. Craig was downstairs, dressed in sweater and trousers and trying to appear cheerful. But his face was dreadfully pale.

Alison went to sit beside him on the sofa and took his hand in hers. He squeezed it and turned a valiant smile in her direction. Even Jenny seemed to know that something momentous was about to happen, and settled at her master's feet, looking up anxiously.

In a tense silence the doctor began to unwind the bandages. It seemed to go on for ever, but at last the final bandage fell away. Craig's eyes stayed closed, and Delia knew that he dreaded opening them, in case his final hope died.

She sat on his other side, and took his hand in hers. 'Come on, darling,' she whispered. 'Take the bull by the horns.'

At last Craig's eyes opened. His head was bent, and nobody could see his face. It was impossible to tell whether he saw or not.

Then a faint smile came over his face. He seemed to focus his attention on Alison's hand, holding his on the left, and Delia's, doing the same on the right. Slowly he raised them to hold them against his face.

For a moment Delia misunderstood. Her heart lurched painfully at what she believed was a gesture seeking comfort. Then his head went up and she saw his smile, broad now, and telling everything.

'Craig?' she said, almost unable to speak. 'Craig, tell me.'

'It's all right,' he said in an awed voice.

Alison gave a shriek of delight that reached the ceiling, and flung her arms about his neck, crying, 'Daddy, Daddy.' Jenny gave a bark.

Craig hugged his daughter back eagerly. 'I can see you, chicken,' he said. 'Let me look at you better.'

She drew back so that he could study her face. 'You're smashing,' he said.

'And Jenny? Isn't she smashing too?'

He looked down at the golden head, the chin resting on his knee. 'Jenny's everything I hoped she would be,' he said.

While he was speaking he kept a tight hold of Delia's hand. Once he glanced at her briefly and she understood the message. There was so much for them to say that couldn't be said now.

They held themselves in check while the doctor gave instructions about future care, which they barely heard. Alison showed him to the door, then tactfully vanished.

Craig took Delia's face between his hands, and looked deeply. Her shining eyes and trembling lips touched his heart more than words could have done.

'I knew,' he said simply. 'All the time I knew you'd look like this. I knew the beauty of your eyes, because I knew your heart. And I'd found your lips for myself...' He brushed his own against them gently. 'But mostly I knew that your face would tell me that you love me. And as long as it says that you will always be beautiful.'

'Even when I'm old and grey?' she asked.

'Until the end of time,' he said softly. 'And that's the greatest beauty in the world.'

In 1999 in Harlequin Romance® marriage is top of the agenda!

Get ready for a great new series by some of our most popular authors, bringing romance to the workplace! This series features gorgeous heroes and lively heroines who discover that mixing business with pleasure can lead to anything...even matrimony!

Books in this series are:

January 1999
Agenda: Attraction! by Jessica Steele

February 1999
Boardroom Proposal by Margaret Way

March 1999
Temporary Engagement by Jessica Hart

April 1999
Beauty and the Boss by Lucy Gordon

May 1999
The Boss and the Baby by Leigh Michaels

From boardroom...to bride and groom!

Available wherever Harlequin books are sold.

Makes any time special ™

If you enjoyed what you just read,
then we've got an offer you can't resist!

Take 2 bestselling
love stories FREE!

Plus get a FREE surprise gift!

Clip this page and mail it to Harlequin Reader Service®

IN U.S.A.	IN CANADA
3010 Walden Ave.	P.O. Box 609
P.O. Box 1867	Fort Erie, Ontario
Buffalo, N.Y. 14240-1867	L2A 5X3

YES! Please send me 2 free Harlequin Romance® novels and my free surprise gift. Then send me 4 brand-new novels every month, which I will receive months before they're available in stores. In the U.S.A., bill me at the bargain price of $2.90 plus 25¢ delivery per book and applicable sales tax, if any*. In Canada, bill me at the bargain price of $3.34 plus 25¢ delivery per book and applicable taxes**. That's the complete price and a savings of over 10% off the cover prices—what a great deal! I understand that accepting the 2 free books and gift places me under no obligation ever to buy any books. I can always return a shipment and cancel at any time. Even if I never buy another book from Harlequin, the 2 free books and gift are mine to keep forever. So why not take us up on our invitation. You'll be glad you did!

116 HEN CNEP
316 HEN CNEQ

Name	(PLEASE PRINT)	
Address	Apt.#	
City	State/Prov.	Zip/Postal Code

* Terms and prices subject to change without notice. Sales tax applicable in N.Y.
** Canadian residents will be charged applicable provincial taxes and GST.
   All orders subject to approval. Offer limited to one per household.
   ® are registered trademarks of Harlequin Enterprises Limited.

HROM99   ©1998 Harlequin Enterprises Limited

Coming Next Month

#3551 MAIL-ORDER MARRIAGE Margaret Way

All that was missing from Matthew Carlyle's life was the right woman to share his Outback cattle-station home. Short on time to socialize, he'd advertized for a wife. City-born Cassandra Sterling had answered him, but how serious about marriage could this poor little rich girl be?

#3552 THE BOSS AND THE BABY Leigh Michaels

Four years ago, Lucas Hudson had dismissed Molly's feelings for him as infatuation—how could she now work for him? She would have to swallow her pride and think of the three-year-old daughter she had to support. But how long would it take Lucas to realize that he'd left Molly with more than a broken heart—that he'd left her with their baby?

Marrying the Boss: From boardroom...to bride and groom!

#3553 UNDERCOVER BABY Rebecca Winters

Diana Rawlins has turned up at the hospital with amnesia and a baby in her arms! She doesn't remember how either of them happened. Her husband, Cal, is determined to get to the bottom of the mystery—especially as that seems to be the only way he can save his marriage!

Love Undercover: Their mission was marriage!

#3554 LOVE & MARRIAGE Betty Neels & Emma Goldrick

Help celebrate Harlequin's fiftieth anniversary in style with this special two-in-one volume from two of our most popular Romance authors.

"MAKING SURE OF SARAH" by Betty Neels

Having fallen in love with Sarah at first sight, Dr. Litrik ter Breukel vowed to go slowly because of her youth and innocence. But perhaps he'd taken things too slowly—it seemed to him that she'd found another man! Now it was up to Sarah to put him right, and it was up to Litrik to propose!

"SOMETHING BLUE" by Emma Goldrick

What could a girl say when her ex-husband turned up out of the blue and asked her to marry him—again? That was the problem facing Marne when Rob suddenly re-proposed. But did he still want only a convenient wife?

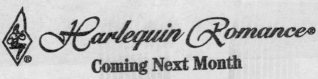

Coming Next Month

#3551 MAIL-ORDER MARRIAGE Margaret Way
All that was missing from Matthew Carlyle's life was the right woman
to share his Outback cattle-station home. Short on time to socialize,
he'd advertized for a wife. City-born Cassandra Sterling had answered
him, but how serious about marriage could this poor little rich girl be?

#3552 THE BOSS AND THE BABY Leigh Michaels
Four years ago, Lucas Hudson had dismissed Molly's feelings for him as
infatuation—how could she now work for him? She would have to
swallow her pride and think of the three-year-old daughter she had to
support. But how long would it take Lucas to realize that he'd left
Molly with more than a broken heart—that he'd left her with their
baby?

Marrying the Boss: *From boardroom...to bride and groom!*

#3553 UNDERCOVER BABY Rebecca Winters
Diana Rawlins has turned up at the hospital with amnesia and a baby
in her arms! She doesn't remember how either of them happened. Her
husband, Cal, is determined to get to the bottom of the mystery—
especially as that seems to be the only way he can save his marriage!

Love Undercover: *Their mission was marriage!*

#3554 LOVE & MARRIAGE Betty Neels & Emma Goldrick
Help celebrate Harlequin's fiftieth anniversary in style with this
special two-in-one volume from two of our most popular
Romance authors.

"MAKING SURE OF SARAH" by Betty Neels
Having fallen in love with Sarah at first sight, Dr. Litrik ter Breukel
vowed to go slowly because of her youth and innocence. But perhaps
he'd taken things too slowly—it seemed to him that she'd found
another man! Now it was up to Sarah to put him right, and it was up
to Litrik to propose!

"SOMETHING BLUE" by Emma Goldrick
What could a girl say when her ex-husband turned up out of the blue
and asked her to marry him—again? That was the problem facing
Marne when Rob suddenly re-proposed. But did he still want only a
convenient wife?